## He Wanted

Needed to hold her. Ye...
as they danced down h...
fragrance fill his head...
skin felt as velvety as i...
breasts to press against him, for her legs to wrap
around his as their bodies merged.

He opened his eyes, needing a distraction, but the
starkly erotic image still hovered, not the least
hazy.

Fast. It had all happened too fast. Which proved
what he felt was infatuation. Which meant, given
time, he could control it.

They had no future together. He'd seen to that
eighteen years ago. To forget for a minute that he
was no ordinary man was foolish.

And Chase Ryan was no fool.

Dear Reader

Spring is in the air and we have a fabulous, fresh line-up from Desire™, including some of your favourite mini-series. Continuing her famous **Tallchiefs** series, bestselling author Cait London brings us sexy **Man of the Month**, Rafe Palladin. He knows fiery Demi Tallchief is his perfect match—but *she* needs a little persuasion. And Lass Small rounds off **The Keepers of Texas** trilogy with love-shy youngest son, Tom Keeper, finally being tempted into matrimony.

Last month we had the *Cinderella Twin*, and now it's her glamorous sister's turn. Jackie Du Marcel falls for a tall, dark businessman in *The Older Man* but why does he appear to be avoiding her? And find out why Chase Ryan is struggling to hide *His Most Scandalous Secret* in the latest story from Susan Crosby.

Finally, Shawna Delacorte brings us a tycoon who discovers he has a secret son, and Carol Grace's heroine inherits a cowboy—whether she wants to or not!

Enjoy them all.

The Editors

# His Most Scandalous Secret

## SUSAN CROSBY

*First published in Great Britain 1999
Silhouette Books, Eton House, 18-24 Paradise Road,
Richmond, Surrey TW9 1SR*

© Susan Bova Crosby 1998

ISBN 0 373 76158 9

22-9904

*Printed and bound in Spain
by Litografia Rosés S.A., Barcelona*

# SUSAN CROSBY

is fascinated by the special and complex communication of courtship, and so she burrows into her office to dream up warm, strong heroes and good-hearted, self-reliant heroines to satisfy her own love of happy endings.

She and her husband have two grown-up sons and live in the Central Valley of California. She spent a mere seven-and-a-half years getting through college and finally earned a B.A. in English a few years ago. She has worked as a synchronized swimming instructor, a personnel interviewer at a toy factory, and a trucking company manager. Involved for many years behind the scenes in a local community theatre, she has made only one stage appearance—as the rear end of a camel! Variety, she says, makes for more interesting novels.

Readers are welcome to write to her at P.O. Box 1836, Lodi, CA 95241, USA.

## Other novels by Susan Crosby

*Silhouette Desire*®

The Mating Game
Almost a Honeymoon
Baby Fever
Wedding Fever
Marriage On His Mind
Bride Candidate No. 9

# One

She was asking for trouble.

Chase Ryan leaned both palms against his office window frame and watched the woman standing on the sidewalk about forty feet away, the bus she'd disembarked from rumbling off in a cloud of diesel smoke as she eyed his building, then the piece of paper she held.

Everything about her was soft, from the long, brunette curls to the swirling skirt that almost reached her ankles. Definitely not the type of woman usually found wandering the street in front of the Wilson Buckley Youth Center of San Francisco, of which Chase was administrator.

And he had the sneaking suspicion that the woman was none other than Tessa Rose, who, barring natural disaster, was the Center's new preschool teacher. If that was the case, she should hop aboard the next bus and go back where she came from. No way was that woman equipped to handle the residents of this neighborhood.

His conscience weighing strong, he briefly considered withdrawing the job offer, although the Center was in dire need of another day care teacher. However, business was business. It wasn't his job to warn people off, but to hire the most qualified applicants.

Not only was Tessa Rose the most qualified, she was the only applicant.

"Hey, Mr. Ryan? You through talkin'?"

Chase had forgotten he was in the middle of a discussion with the thirteen-year-old who came up beside him. He glanced at the boy. "I'm sorry, Luis. My mind wandered."

His gaze returned involuntarily to look out the window as the woman made her way closer. His impression of softness deepened as the July afternoon breeze lifted her hair away from her face. A high-collared pink blouse hugged her breasts. Her floral-printed skirt molded born-to-carry-babies hips and endless legs.

Not one original thought crossed his mind. She was a fish out of water. A man could lose himself in her. She was the kind of woman you took home to meet your mother.

"Can I go now, Mr. Ryan?"

He didn't look at the boy. "If you're called in a second time for breaking the same rule, you forfeit your membership. I don't want to see that happen, not after you were on the waiting list so long."

"I didn't know that *damn* was a swear word, Mr. Ryan. Honest." Luis pressed his hands to the window. "Hey, isn't that Stone Man?"

Chase spotted the teenager tracking the woman who had no business being in this neighborhood alone. She stopped in front of the youth center and rummaged through her purse, the oversize quilted bag an easy target for a kid who took what he wanted.

Chase twisted the window lock open. Before he could shove the sash up to alert her, the kid made his move—and the woman flattened him facedown across the hood of the nearest car, locking his arm behind his back. Her body jerked as she applied more pressure every so often. She spoke directly into his ear.

"Holy—" Luis gulped. "I mean, wow. Did you see that, Mr. Ryan? Shoot. Look at Stone Man go! Je—I mean, can you believe it? Is she one of those Amazons we studied in school?"

"Not tall enough," Chase murmured, his awe less vocal than Luis's but just as complete. He finished shoving open the window. "Need any help there, Miss?" he called.

"Thanks, but I'm fine." She dusted off her hands as Stone Man rounded the corner and disappeared. "You wouldn't happen to be Chase Ryan?"

He nodded, still amazed by what she'd done.

"I'm Tessa Rose. I have an appointment with you." She glanced at her watch, then back at him. Her smile was brilliant, blinding. Lethal. "I seem to be a minute late."

"I'll save us both some time, then, Miss Rose. If you want the job, you've got it."

"I want the job."

"Come up and we'll talk details."

She swung her bag over her shoulder and bounded up the stairs to the Center, enthusiasm in every step. How long until that spirit fizzled and burned out? He'd seen it dozens of times. He hated that it would happen to someone as fresh and full of passion as Miss Tessa Rose.

She stepped into his office, that megawatt smile in place.

"Hi. Who just flew by me faster than a speeding bullet?" she asked, looking down the hall for a second.

"That was Luis, who happened to witness your performance. Your reputation will be firmly established within fifteen minutes, Miss Rose." Even her name was soft. He indicated a chair to her, then moved behind his desk and took a seat. "Nice job handling yourself out there."

"Thanks."

"I take it you saw him coming."

"The minute I stepped off the bus. I also knew I couldn't avoid him. He was too close." She leaned forward. "Do I really have the job?"

"Our meeting was just a formality. The day care director, Chandra, wants you, and your references are glowing, as I'm sure you're aware." He tipped his chair back. "It's my policy to run down the rules with everyone, whether staff, parent or child."

"Because everyone is more comfortable when they know what's expected of them, and what the consequences are when they fail to meet expectation."

"Exactly." Baby blue eyes, he noted, with laugh lines fanning from the corners. He knew she was twenty-nine, so the creases hadn't come only from age. "Why do you want to work here, Miss Rose?"

She crossed her legs and relaxed into the chair. "Why wouldn't I want to work here, Mr. Ryan?"

"This isn't the safest neighborhood in the city."

"It's my understanding that you run an orderly facility. Within the walls, I expect I'll be very safe. As for coming and going, you already saw how little problem that poses."

"Your last job was at the day care center for the Schuman Corporation." He knew the details of her résumé without looking. "Advantaged kids who probably were fed breakfast and clothed in the latest fashions before being dropped off. Parents who probably worked eight to five, and maybe even visited the child during their lunch hour."

"Your point, Mr. Ryan?"

He watched her foot bounce impatiently, sending the fabric of her skirt rippling. A fresh, flowery scent made its way across the desk. Roses? She should be tending a garden herself in some picket-fenced little house somewhere, not fending off small-time teenage hoodlums. He gave her one last chance. "You'll see things here you'll wish you hadn't, want to make changes in the children's lives that can't be made. You may be trained to defend your body from harm, but what about your heart?"

"Are you trying to scare me off?" For the first time a completely serious expression settled on her face. "I grew up not far from here, Mr. Ryan. Although the neighborhood has changed some, I doubt much will surprise me. I've read your mission statement and the rules that you make the kids sign and the forms the parents complete, agreeing not only to cooperate but to participate. I spent an afternoon working beside Chandra, and I was here when the children were picked up. I know who they are and what kind of life they lead. I'm not as naive as you seem to think. However, I don't see anything wrong with wanting to do what I can to make things better for the children in this neighborhood. I believe that is your purpose, as well.''

"How long a commitment are you willing to make?"

"I know these kids need stable adult role models. I'll be here."

Ten seconds of silence followed her response. Their gazes had locked the moment she'd entered his office and hadn't disconnected once. He finally looked away, but only long enough to pull some papers out of a file drawer and pass them to her. "Welcome aboard."

"Thanks." She plucked a pen and clipboard from her Mary Poppins bag and began to complete the legal documents.

"What'd you say to the boy when you had him spread-eagled on the car?"

"I offered to rearrange some of his anatomy, free of charge— in language he could understand, of course." She flashed a smile. "He seemed to take me seriously. So, who is this Wilson Buckley the Center is named for?"

"You'll meet him. Everyone calls him Sarge." He watched her fill in the blanks on the W-4 form. "He retired from the police force nineteen years ago."

"Which explains why his name doesn't ring any bells. I didn't have any brushes with the law until I was, oh, seventeen or so."

"Speeding ticket?"

She tossed him a mischievous glance. "A sit-in at my high school, protesting the cafeteria food. A bunch of us got hauled in. My parents were not amused."

"I don't imagine they were. Did the situation change at the school after that?"

"Sure. After I graduated."

"So, you made a difference for those who followed. Was that enough for you?"

"Well...*no*."

Ambitious, determined and just self-centered enough. Good qualities for working at the Center, Chase thought.

"After that experience, I decided maybe I should become a cop," she said. "I liked the way they handled the whole situation."

"Why didn't you?"

"I kind of have a problem with guns. They pretty much scare me to death." She held up a hand. "I know. I see the question in your eyes." She leaned forward, intent on making her point. "I really thought I could do the job without having to use a weapon other than my mind. Sadly, I didn't pass the psychological exam. Too high on idealism."

He could have predicted that about her himself. "I'm sorry your career plans were shattered, Miss Rose."

"I'm over it." She cocked her head. "Do we call each other Mister and Miss forever?"

"Not when we're alone...Tessa. The kids are required to, however."

"Good."

A long, lustrous curl drifted over her shoulder as she wrote, settling on her breast, quivering as she penned her answer to the who-do-we-call-in-an-emergency question. He clenched his teeth. Hiring Miss Tessa Rose was probably going to be the second biggest mistake in his thirty-two years of life. His gaze returned to that lucky curl. He wanted to wrap it around his finger, let his hand rest against the beautiful curve of flesh below it and slowly trace the tempting shape.

He pushed himself out of his chair. "I'll be back."

Tessa watched him stride from the room, stirring the air, disturbing her papers. She tapped her pen against her lips as she stared blindly at the form. In her search for information about the

Center, she'd learned that Chase Ryan had a reputation for uncompromising expectation, but she hadn't realized that uncompromising meant *hard*. Most people smiled in return for one offered. Not him. Not even the tiniest curve of his lips to be social, to be civilized.

And yet she didn't feel any threat behind the edges and angles that defined him—the square, determined jaw; the strong, powerful body; the smoky gray eyes, fierce with never-give-in resolution. Only his hair hinted at anything remotely soft about him, although the dark hue seemed to match his personality. But the length surprised her, the ends caressing his shirt collar as they did.

Word on the street was that he lived by strict, self-imposed laws, and she could see for herself that he wouldn't be easily reformed.

Her pen clattered as it hit the floor. Why had the thought even entered her head? Yes, she'd wanted to meet him, to understand him, but why in the world would she want to change him? Certainly she wanted to see a smile relax his face; however, she didn't believe in forcing people to change. She'd learned from experience that it never worked.

"Something wrong?"

He had come up quietly behind her, or she'd been so lost in her thoughts, she just hadn't heard him return. His eyes held a touch of concern.

"I dropped my pen." It was a stupid thing to say—as if she couldn't pick up a fallen pen from the floor. His hesitation asked a question into the void, but he crouched and retrieved the pen, then passed it to her.

Her hand brushed his. Her gaze flew to meet his. Nothing, nothing like this had ever happened to her. Someone must have switched on a spotlight inside her body. Heat and light filled her. Burned her. Perspiration pulled her clothes closer to her skin. Her throat tightened.

He removed his hand but stayed crouched beside her.

"Don't be afraid of me." His voice soothed. Calmed. Tempted.
*Tempted?*

What happened? She'd been in control, completely in control.
She knew who he was. What kind of man he was—now and
before. She was not afraid of him. Surely just his touch couldn't—

"Can I get you something? A glass of water?"

The phone rang, a reprieve for her as he leaned across his desk
to answer it, although he watched her the whole time. She gripped
the pen and finished completing the forms.

When he hung up, she passed him the papers and stood, tugging her purse strap over her shoulder.

"Can you start tomorrow?" he asked.

She made herself answer. "Yes, I can."

"Chandra said you were willing to take the late shift with the
two- and three-year-olds."

"That's right. Yours is one of the few day care centers I know
of that stays open until eight at night. I'm not really a morning
person, so it works out great for me."

He glanced at her paperwork. "Your address has changed since
you first applied."

"I found a new apartment nearby. I'm moving in today."
Small, but hers. All hers, for the first time in her life. Independence, hard-won and appreciated. Tonight was her first night on
her own.

"People still look out for each other along that block." He
paused. "Are you sure you're all right, Tessa? Maybe I should
take you home."

"I'm fine. Really. I'll see you tomorrow."

He scanned her face once more. "Don't be surprised if the
boys here give you a wide berth for a while and the girls start
hanging around, offering to help in the day care area when they're
not even signed up to work. Your legend will precede you. You
might even consider teaching a self-defense class before the summer's up."

"One isn't already offered?"

"It's offered, but a new slant is always good, particularly because you're a woman and you're not a cop. Be extra alert when you leave here, Tessa. You humiliated the boy—Stone Man is what he's called, by the way—and I don't know whether he'll avoid you now because of it or find some way to get even."

"I'm always careful, but thanks for the advice." She smiled her farewell and left.

He moved to watch her from his window. After a few seconds he could see her make her way down the stairs, using the handrail this time, taking a step at a time. She didn't wait for a bus, but headed the opposite direction, toward where her new apartment was located.

He should have insisted on taking her home. He didn't know Stone Man except by reputation. He'd never come to the Center, not even for events open to the public. Chase would check out the kid's record, see how much of a threat he posed.

Long after Tessa disappeared from sight, Chase stayed at the window. Something had triggered a change in her. A delayed reaction to the confrontation with the teenager? Or was it himself? His friend Ariel told him once that he was the meanest-looking man she'd ever seen.

Except to shave and comb his hair once a day, he didn't look in the mirror. He needed no reminders of who he was. What simmered inside him all the time was reminder enough, and kept him focused on his purpose. People did sometimes cast wary glances his way on the street. He always figured it was from natural caution, not because he appeared threatening.

Had Tessa been afraid of him?

She disturbed him, as well. Her softness teased him with promises he tried not to visualize. But even now he could smell her perfume and picture the womanly shape of her. A lot of power was packed into that body, some in physical strength, more in temptation.

He'd win this battle, though. Just as he'd won every other battle of temptation he'd fought.

As she unlocked her door, Tessa sighed, glad to be home. The walk from the Center to her apartment was barely five blocks, but she'd been constantly on alert. She wondered what the teenager's real name was and why he'd been dubbed Stone Man. He couldn't have been more than fifteen. So young to be living such an old life.

Her journey had also been reconnaissance, as she memorized her surroundings and checked out escape paths, getting to know the route from home to work. After the emotional scene with her family this morning—her last day living under their roof—and her bewildering response to Chase Ryan, she needed time alone.

And if she'd shut her door just two seconds sooner, she would have found sanctuary. Instead, her across-the-hall neighbor opened his door.

"Hi, Tess."

She did not like being called Tess. She'd told him so yesterday when he'd shortened her name upon introduction. Obviously, he either didn't listen or didn't care. Or maybe because he used a shortened version of his own name, he did so with others. Not wanting to alienate a neighbor, though, she managed a smile for the thirty-something man who'd helped her father carry her sofa bed up the stairs.

"Hello, Norm."

"Get settled in okay?"

"Yes, thanks. I still have some boxes to unpack, though, so if you'll excuse me."

From behind him, a young woman slipped out of his apartment, planting a kiss on his lips as she passed by. "See you later, honey." She gave Tessa the once-over before sending a distinctly *He's mine* admonition with her eyes, silent and direct. "I'm Marcy. I live downstairs in 1B."

Relieved that Norm was involved with someone, Tessa offered her hand. "Tessa Rose."

Marcy must have believed the *Message received* answer in Tessa's return gaze and abrupt handshake, because she visibly relaxed. She nodded, then hurried down the stairs.

"Your girlfriend?" she asked Norm, who hadn't shut his door yet.

"Yep." He tucked his hands in his back pockets. "Anything you need help with?"

"Everything's fine, but thank you for asking. Bye." She retreated before he could reply. Resting against her closed door, she surveyed her domain. *Small* was hardly the word for it. One medium-size room, a utilitarian bathroom, a one-person kitchen with counter bar and one surprisingly roomy walk-in closet with enough space for her meager belongings.

It was hers, though, from the sofa bed where she would sit and sleep to the four place settings of dinnerware she had yet to unpack. Twenty-nine years old and finally living on her own. No more accounting for where she was every second of the day. No more listening to her mother worry aloud about the potential dangers facing them everywhere. No more seeing her father age day by day.

No more enduring her brother sitting in his wheelchair by the front window, watching the world go by, venturing out once a month or so, otherwise living in a television world.

He hadn't said anything when she announced she'd found her own apartment and was moving out, but she figured he was glad to have her gone. Her pleas to do something for himself always fell on deaf ears. He hadn't done anything to improve his life for years. And she'd taken all the whining she could bear about his bad luck.

She pushed away from the door, stripped down to her underwear right there in the middle of the room and tugged on a T-shirt and cutoffs so that she could finish putting her home in order. She felt a little wicked going braless, even though she knew no one would catch her at it, but she draped her bra over the door-knob, anyway. If someone did come, she could always put it on fast.

The phone rang just as she started scrubbing the bathtub. Peeling off her rubber gloves as she went, she hurried into the living room.

Breathless, she picked it up on the fourth ring. "Hello?"

"This is Chase Ryan."

Tessa sank onto the couch. "Hi."

"I wanted to make sure you got home all right."

The sound of his voice did things to her. Made her shiver. Made her unconfined breasts feel strangely fuller.

"Tessa? Are you okay?"

"Fine. I'm fine." His voice, the memory of his serious face and the admiration he hadn't hidden for the way she'd handled Stone Man streaked through her mind. She wasn't used to being treated as a capable adult. He couldn't have any idea how much it meant to her that he had.

"No sign of the teenager?" he asked.

"None. Thank you for your concern, though."

"I'm having a friend in the police department check him out, just to be sure. He's fairly new to the area, and he's gained a reputation fast with the kids around here."

"Is he the kind of boy you try to get involved at the Center? Do you seek out the troubled kids, Chase, and set them on a different path?"

"I do what I can. Sometimes I succeed."

*Sometimes I don't.* The unspoken words carried resignation. How had she become connected to him so fast that she could hear what he didn't say?

*Because what's forbidden is always more of an allure.*

Tessa ignored her thoughts and stretched out on the sofa, letting all the sensations settle in. She was hot and cold and shaky and...alive. Maybe it was just reaction to her success—her emancipation from her old life and inauguration to her new one.

Regardless, Chase Ryan was a bonus she hadn't counted on. Now she had to figure out what to do about it. He needed her— or someone like her.

And her family would die if she—

"Tessa? Where'd you go?"

"Um, I was just thinking that maybe you could go ahead and schedule a self-defense class for the weekend. Might as well capitalize on my current fame."

"I'll get on it right away."

She didn't move after she hung up the phone. Instead, she closed her eyes and imagined his face. An old image superimposed itself for a moment, then got shoved behind the newer one without effort. She'd entered into a risky business. The route she'd intended to take no longer seemed the right one. No longer made sense. No longer seemed plausible, even.

Because in all of her plans, she hadn't counted on there being so much to lose.

# Two

Chase knew the minute that Tessa arrived at the Center for her first day at work. He didn't leave his office to greet her, but let her go to the day care center on her own.

The Center hummed with talk of her. She'd attained sainthood with just one miracle.

"Good morning."

He turned from the window. She hadn't gone to day care first, after all. There she stood, in a denim jumper, a baby blue T-shirt that matched her eyes, and sneakers painted with teddy bears and balloons. Head to toe, she looked like a preschool teacher.

"Morning," he said. "Are you ready for this?"

"You bet. I hardly slept last night, I was so excited." She leaned against the door frame, as if she had all the time in the world, not the three minutes she really did have before she should be reporting to Chandra.

"I posted a sign-up sheet for your self-defense class," he said. "It hadn't been up an hour before it was half-full. I expect that by the end of the day, it'll be a sellout."

"You can schedule two or three sessions if you want, in order to fill the demand. I'll be concentrating more on awareness than technique, and smaller groups would work better. I'd also prefer coed."

"We pretty much do everything coed here. I don't believe in segregating them. The only way the Center can be successful is to have everyone a part of everything, like a family. We preach tolerance. We try to elevate everyone's self-esteem. If we don't, we lose the girls to single motherhood and the boys to gangs."

Soft. Her eyes were so soft as she smiled at him. Tempted him. As if to say that he could share with her, things he'd never shared.

"I like your philosophy, Mr. Ryan," she said.

"It's not mine alone. It's what's been proven to work." He walked around his desk and came up beside her, close enough to smell her perfume, close enough to thread his fingers through her curls, if he'd wanted. If he'd been allowed such a luxury. "I'll walk you to day care."

"I can manage. I just wanted to say good morning. It's important to greet people, don't you think? And to let them know when you're leaving."

So—he'd been put on notice that she would be saying hello and goodbye every day. That she would seek him out. That he should seek her out if he was leaving for some reason.

"Are we allowed to hug?" she asked.

His hands curled into fists. "What?"

"Do the adults hug the children here? There are so many rules these days. Sick, sad rules because people cry abuse so easily."

"Oh." Disappointment swept through him before he could squelch it. He'd already locked on to the image of him holding her. Her holding him. "We encourage appropriate physical contact."

"Now there's a textbook answer." Her eyes danced merrily. She feathered the hair on his arm with her fingertips until his skin rose in bumps. "Is that appropriate?"

"Try it on one of the boys and you may have to use every self-defense technique you know."

She tossed her hair. "But I'm safe with you?"

"Not safe at all, Miss Rose."

Her eyes flickered with interest. He never flirted with women. Never. But she was digging deeper into him than anyone had and finding a place he hadn't known existed.

"*Safe* is for wimps," she said.

"And we all agree you're not a wimp."

"Oh, I have my moments." Her hand drifted away. "I'm sure I'll see you occasionally throughout the day."

"Count on it."

A smile came and went. "I will."

He let out a long, slow breath as she walked away, leaving a trail of fragrance and an eyeful of softly swaying hips. He swallowed, hungry for her, at the same time wary of the hunger.

Maybe it was time to take his first vacation in nine years.

The last cherubic face had been washed and the last squirming body covered with a blanket in the nap room before Tessa found time to draw a deep breath. She turned a comical expression on Chandra, the day care director.

"Lively bunch," Tessa said. In her charge were twenty preschoolers and four aides, an excellent balance. Still, learning their names and personalities made a person a little foggy for a while. And she'd only been at work a few hours.

"Thank goodness for the teenagers who volunteer to help. During the school year, we only have two aides each. It can be overwhelming," Chandra said, looking at her watch. "I wonder where Dodger is. He should have been here an hour ago."

"Who's Dodger?"

"He delivers our food order three times a week. We just qualified for a huge grant that will allow us more fresh fruits and vegetables and enough milk, cereal and pasta to feed this small army. Dodger's been getting here later and later, though. Guess

I'm gonna have to complain to his boss.'' She pushed herself out of the chair. ''Grab some lunch while you can, Tessa. I'll be on the phone awhile.''

Tuna sandwich had never tasted so good, Tessa thought as she leaned her head against the back of her chair, closed her eyes and chewed. She liked the environment of this place, so different from the Schuman Corporation, where everything was updated continually, the latest toys and computers purchased frequently to entertain and teach. Here, however, they made do with castoffs that had been cleaned up and lots of homemade toys and games. And the kids were gems. Unspoiled, full of giggles, happy for the attention.

A sixth sense told her that someone was watching her. She took her time opening her eyes, knowing that it was Chase.

It wasn't. A ponytailed young man stood in the doorway, a blue baseball cap perched backward on his head, a handcart loaded with boxes in front of him.

''You the new teach?'' he asked, coming into the room, heading toward the door that led to the kitchen. ''I'm Dodger.''

She stood, uneasy. She didn't know how long he'd been watching her while she was lost in her own thoughts. ''I'll tell Mrs. Moore you're here.''

''Not to worry, babe. I know where I'm goin'.''

''My name is Miss Rose.''

He eyed her coolly, then shrugged and turned away. ''Whatever. You want to come along and sign for this stuff?''

A masculine voice answered, ''I will.''

Chase came into the room, his expression fiercer than usual. ''Thank you, Miss Rose. I'll take care of this. Finish your lunch.''

She could hear the men talking as she sat again. She wanted to creep closer to the kitchen, to hear what Chase was telling the young man. Dodger came out in a minute, winked at her, then pushed the handcart ahead of him.

''He'll be back with more,'' Chase said, leaning against the doorway. ''I'll stay until he's done.''

"Okay."

"I explained the rules. No one swears, no one speaks disrespectfully to another. He's not part of the Center, but while he's here, he's expected to conform."

"He doesn't look like a conformist," Tessa said, smiling at his paternal attitude. "Care for a sandwich? I've got plenty to share."

She could see him automatically start to say no, then his answer eased into the affirmative. He sat beside her, accepting the tuna sandwich. She shoved some chips his way and opened a large plastic bag filled with oatmeal-and-raisin cookies.

"How is your day going?" he asked.

"Great. The kids are amazing."

"In what way?"

"Nothing bores them, for one thing. And they share pretty well, considering their ages. The teenagers who are helping out are terrific, too. I'll be sorry to lose them when school starts."

"You'll have more help than the early-in-the-day teachers because once school lets out for the day, the kids start piling in. Everyone has to pay to be a member here, and if they can't afford it, they work off the equivalent in time. We always have help. We count on it. Did you make the cookies?"

"Mmm-hmm. I didn't have any champagne, so I launched my new apartment by making cookies."

Dodger returned and made a straight line for the kitchen. As he came back through, Tessa offered him some cookies, as well. She was aware of Chase angling her way, stretching out his legs and crossing his ankles, as if there for the duration. She wondered if he was aware of what a mark of ownership his actions were.

Dodger grabbed a handful of cookies. "Thanks, Miss Rose."

"You're welcome, Mr. Dodger."

He laughed, then his gaze slid to Chase, effectively ending the conversation.

"You are formidable," Tessa said to Chase when Dodger left.

"Am I?"

She smiled. "You're a natural."

"I'm not, actually."

"Formidable, or a natural?"

"Either."

"Yes, you are. This is your kingdom."

He wadded his sandwich wrap into a ball and tossed it into a wastebasket. "The Center is a democracy. I just oversee it."

"You rule it."

He shook his head. "That's not true. Ten people make up the board of directors. Of those ten, five are teenagers. The remaining five aren't politicians or civic leaders but people from this community, people who have a vested interest in the success of this venture."

"But ultimately you have the final word." She watched his bland expression for any nuance of change.

"I've only intervened once in a board decision. The kids wanted to purchase some televisions. They'd even swayed two of the adults to their side. I said no."

"Why?"

"Because they can watch television at home. I want them busy here. Not just physically, with sports, but mentally. There's a quiet room for them to do homework or read. They form discussion groups, and I don't put limits on the subjects. The fact they're communicating, especially with each other, is what's important. Peer counseling is critical. They learn that they can deal with their problems using their minds, not their fists and certainly not weapons. I can't tell you how many times a child has confided in another child here. Some of them have learned the social service system better than I have. They do their own referrals. It works. And I usually catch the ones that fall through the cracks."

"Chandra told me that you have a master's degree in child psychology."

He nodded. "And I counsel when and where I can. But the kids respond best to their peers. I not only allow it, I encourage it."

The sound of a cranky child cut short Tessa's response. They both looked up as the aide who monitored the nap room came in carrying a fussy two-year-old.

"Sorry to disturb your lunch, Miss Rose, but Christa woke up crying. I can't get her to tell me if something hurts."

"Thank you, Jennifer. Come here, sweetheart."

The toddler had other ideas. She hurled herself in Chase's direction, trying to escape Jennifer's hold. "Want *you.*"

Tessa shrugged as he lifted his brows in silent question. He was familiar to the children, and she was new. She didn't expect them to come to her yet, and certainly wouldn't force it.

He took Christa into his arms. She cuddled against him, sniffling dramatically, jamming her thumb in her mouth, her tears slowing.

"Magic touch," Jennifer said to Tessa as she walked away. "The kids love him."

Tessa watched him calm the softly hiccuping little girl and knew exactly why no child would fear him. He spoke to Christa in hushed tones, the gentle huskiness accompanied by an equally comforting touch of his hand, large and soothing, as he stroked her long, dark hair and tiny back.

He may not smile, but he brought contentment. He was a man people could confide in, knowing their secret was safe. His word was his bond, integrity his covenant. All the research she'd done on him indicated it. Now she could see for herself. Children were the ultimate barometer of a person's character.

Chase Ryan was genuine.

He met Tessa's gaze with a questioning one. She didn't know what he'd seen in her expression—too much had passed through her head in a brief period of time. She smiled at him, the only answer she could give.

"She's asleep," he said. "I'll put her down."

"Thank you."

He looked at Tessa a moment longer. Then, incredibly, he cupped the side of her head, his palm resting against her hair, his fingertips barely touching her scalp, his thumb brushing her cheek. Had she looked as needy as Christa?

"Let me know if Dodger gives you any trouble, Tessa."

She let out the breath she'd been holding, then crossed her arms as he took his hand away. "So, that's how you rule so effectively."

"Meaning?"

"Oh, you tricky man, you. You lure with touch, then you give orders. You figure while I'm mesmerized, I'll agree to anything. Nicely done, Mr. Ryan."

"I'm not that calculated."

"Then your instincts are exceptional."

"Maybe we could talk about it over dinner sometime."

She liked that he'd surprised himself with the invitation, for clearly he had. His expression closed up instantly—too late, of course, but a shutdown nonetheless. "I'd love to," she said simply. "Name the day."

She'd never thought a person's frown endearing before. His tugged at her heart, which was already fluttering from his surprisingly tender touch and the intensity of his stormy gray gaze.

"I'll get back to you," he said.

Tessa smiled as he left the room with Christa. What a fascinating man. Strong-willed, devoted to his work, definitely a leader and yet vulnerable, too. She didn't know which part of him attracted her more. Or maybe it was the contradictions that were so enticing.

Dinner with Chase? A personal relationship with him certainly hadn't been in her plans when she first applied for the job, but she couldn't deny its appeal now. Who would have thought it?

Late that night Chase locked the dead bolt behind him, then climbed the stairs to his second-floor apartment over the Center. Ten o'clock and all's well—except his peace of mind.

Dinner. Where had that invitation come from?

Yes, he was attracted to Tessa. But he'd been attracted to

women before and been able to control the direction of a relationship. With Tessa, he found himself saying and doing things
he couldn't predict and certainly hadn't planned.

He flipped on the light switch as he rounded the corner at the
top of the stairs, illuminating his living room. Some of his friends
would shout hallelujah. He'd often been accused of being too
controlled—Sarge's word. Les said he was hopeless. Sebastian
called him clueless. But what were friends for if not to tell you
the truth about yourself?

Controlled, hopeless, clueless. And Tessa's description—formidable. Not that it fazed the soft, fragrant, cookie baker who
made him yearn for things he'd scratched off his wish list years
ago. His commitment to his purpose was complete—no child
would experience what he'd experienced, not if he had anything
to say about it. And dividing himself between his commitment of
the past eighteen years and the temptation that Tessa represented
now just wouldn't work. Both would suffer if he fragmented his
attention.

He didn't think Tessa would settle for second place. Nor should
she.

He tossed his keys on the kitchen counter, picked up the phone
and dialed.

"O'Keefe."

"What'd you get on Stone Man?"

"Geez, Chase. Give me a break, will you? I'm a detective, not
a miracle worker. I've been chasing bad guys all day and couldn't
get to it."

He eased onto a sturdy bar stool. "This is important, Les.
Tessa's life could be at risk."

"I'm right in the middle of the first date I've had in months.
I'll get to it ASAP, I promise."

"Tomorrow."

Les sighed, a pretty good indication that Chase was testing their
eighteen-year friendship. "All right. All right. Tomorrow."

"So, Les, are you wearing a dress and everything tonight?"

''Go to heck, Ryan.''

''Before you slam the phone down,'' he said quickly, ''check out a guy named Dodger, too, would you? He works at the food bank. I want to know his background.''

''Why?''

*Because I didn't like the way he looked at Tessa today.* ''He's in and out several times a week. Something about him bothers me.''

''I'll see what I can find out.''

''Thanks, Les. I appreciate it.''

''But don't call me, okay? I'll call you when I have some information.''

''Tomorrow.''

''*Tomorrow.*''

The phone line went dead.

Grabbing a couple of plums and the remainder of Tessa's oatmeal-and-raisin cookies, which she'd left with him when she'd said good night, Chase turned out the light and wandered into his bedroom. His walls were lined with cement-block and woodplank bookshelves, filled with everything from textbooks to bestsellers. They were his indulgence, his one luxury and were organized systematically so that he could put his hands on any book he wanted easily. The few people who'd been in the room always stared at the minilibrary.

He stripped and climbed in bed with his snack and a book on inner-city youth. Before long, he set the book aside. He bit into a plum, the tangy juice and sweet flesh filling his mouth as he contemplated the ceiling—and Tessa.

Most of the women he knew were either single mothers struggling just to get by, or social workers embittered by the system that tied their hands, or, as in Les's case, a police detective who saw the worst of human beings day in and day out. Women worn out by the pressure of just getting by. But survivors. He'd always sympathized with them and admired that they got through each day without breaking. Usually, the stronger the woman, the more he admired her.

And yet...there was Tessa Rose. Strong, yes. Physically, anyway. He didn't know enough about her to know if her character was as strong, although he suspected as much. But she was soft, too. Temptingly soft.

He plucked a cookie from the bag and bit into it, its sweet raisins and chewy texture a sensual experience for the man whose most gourmet meal that week consisted of scrambled eggs and salsa, wrapped in a tortilla. Easy and cheap. That was his motto in the kitchen.

A homemade cookie was a rarity, either a Christmas gift or a cooking project in the Center's kitchen.

He looked at the bedside clock, debated a moment, then picked up the phone and dialed the number he'd already memorized.

Tessa answered with a tentative hello.

"It's Chase. I hope I'm not calling too late."

She laughed. "I'm just so relieved it's not my mother."

"Did I wake you?"

"Heavens, no. I'm a night owl. I've been doing some prep work for a craft project for tomorrow."

"I've been thinking about dinner." *How we shouldn't take the chance,* he thought. *How mixing business and pleasure is never a wise move.* "How about Saturday, after you give the self-defense class?"

"That would be great."

*He just wouldn't kiss her good night. Then things wouldn't get complicated.* "Do you like Mexican food?"

"My favorite."

*He wouldn't even hold her hand.* "Good."

"Chase?"

*They'd just talk. Get to know each other. Try to bring in some reality to dim the fantasy that had built too fast.* "Yeah?"

"No one is forcing you to do this, you know."

"Meaning?"

"Meaning you sound like someone has a gun to your head. If you've decided that you don't want to go out with me, I'll understand. I guess."

Ah, a graceful way out. She was perceptive and generous. This could be the end of it, no questions asked. It never had to come up again. "No one forces me to do anything, Tessa."

*Good goin', Ryan. Come across like some Neanderthal. That's just what every woman wants in her life.*

"I'm sure they don't," she said.

A muffled noise punctuated the silence that followed.

"Are you laughing at me, Miss Rose?" he asked, strongly suspicious of the sound.

"No." She choked a little. "Yes."

"Why?" He knew why. He knew exactly why. What an idiot he was. Why did he become like an adolescent with her?

He knew the answer to that, too.

"I really like you, Chase."

"But?"

"No *but*. I've never met a man like you."

"Is that a problem for you?"

"It might be, at some point. But for now, I'm just enjoying it."

"What are you concerned about, Tessa?"

"This is the first time I've been on my own, which seems amazing, I know, given my age. I can't mess it up, Chase."

"And I'm a threat to your independence?"

"Yes."

He waited for her to expand on the answer. Was he just supposed to make his own assumptions about her meaning?

"Chase?"

"Yeah."

"Maybe I'm a threat to you, as well."

"No maybe about it."

"Good night," she said softly, then hung up without waiting for his response.

He dropped the receiver and pressed his palms to his closed eyes. He wanted her beside him. Needed to hold her. Yearned to touch her soft curls as they danced down her back. Craved to have her fragrance fill his head. Hungered to know if her skin felt as velvety as it looked. Ached for her breasts to press against him, for her legs to wrap around his as their bodies merged.

He opened his eyes, needing a distraction, but the starkly erotic image still hovered, not the least hazy.

Fast. It'd all happened too fast. Which qualified what he felt as infatuation. Which meant, given time, he could control it.

They had no future together. He'd seen to that eighteen years ago. To forget even for a minute that he wasn't a normal man was foolish.

And he was no fool.

# Three

———

**"H**ow many of you have been victims of violence?"

Tessa looked around the room at the hands raised in response to her question. She'd decided to run separate classes based on age. This group was all teenagers. In this area of the city it explained why so many hands were up.

"How many of you had any kind of warning?"

Only a couple this time. Probably home violence, Tessa decided, a threat carried out.

"How many of you felt helpless?"

The hands came up again. She came around to the front of the podium, removing the barrier between them.

"The purpose of this class is to prevent you from being a victim. I'm not going to show you fancy moves, because they rarely work, especially if you have only a split second to react. What I will show you is how to defend yourself well enough to escape."

"Miss Rose?"

"Yes, Luis?"

"That was some fancy move you put on Stone Man."

Tessa had anticipated the comment. She glanced at Chase, who leaned against the back wall watching her, a gray-haired man beside him. The infamous Sarge, unless she missed her guess.

"That's a good point, Luis. However, I was prepared for him. Because I'm always aware of who and what is around me, I knew he was probably going to try to grab my purse. I also knew I couldn't escape it, because he was too close."

"How'd you know he was gonna grab it?"

"He slowed down when he saw me. He eyed my bag. I knew what was coming. I stopped at a place on the street where I was sure I could handle him. The second he reached out, I grabbed him. Before he knew it, he was hugging the hood of a car. Yes, I've learned the self-defense moves, but more importantly, I've learned to see what's ahead, what could hurt me and how to make sure it doesn't happen.

"That's what I want you to learn. That, and how to get away. There's nothing tricky about it. There's also a chance you could get hurt. However, your goal is to get away, and you may have to fight back. But your injuries will probably be less than what your attacker had in mind for you."

Every gaze was focused on her. She didn't know whether to be pleased that they sat so attentively or sad that their lives necessitated the class at all.

"Okay. I'll need some volunteers to act the roles of the criminals, preferably boys." At the instant vocal response, she said "I'm not being sexist. This is as realistic as I can make it. Part of the allure of crime for males is their power over females. Women don't commit violent crimes in anywhere near the same numbers."

"And guys are stronger," one of the girls called out as several boys shuffled to the front of the classroom.

Tessa smiled. "Depends on the situation. But we'll deal with that when we get to it. We're going out of the classroom for a few minutes. Mr. Ryan? Would you take over, please?"

He nodded and headed to the front of the class. As he passed by, he grabbed her. Tessa reacted instantly and automatically. Shouting, she pretended to make two quick, debilitating moves, then she turned and ran, screaming. He huddled.

Silence filled the room. The shock on the kids' faces faded when she stopped at the podium and looked at them. They started to chatter amongst themselves. She raised her voice to be heard.

"Mr. Ryan and I set that up ahead of time, although I didn't know when or what he was going to do. I wanted to be as surprised as possible. He did surprise me—" she looked his way "—because I expected him to wait until later in the class. Now let's go over what I just did."

"She came darn close to hurting me, even pretending," Chase said. "Her scream really caught me off guard, and her strength, as well. I thought I was the one in control, but she proved me wrong immediately. I forgot my own plans."

Most of the kids stood to get a closer look as Tessa moved beside Chase and continued her lecture.

"You might be tempted to carry a weapon of some sort, but remember—a weapon can be taken away and used against you. So, you need to use weapons that they can't take. Your fingers. Hands. Elbows. Your feet and knees. I'll show you later."

She looked up at Chase, mentally measuring his height. He stared back, his eyes almost silver in hue. "You're what, six inches—" She stopped, realizing how he might interpret her question. "Um—"

"Seven," he said under his breath.

"Um, Mr. Ryan is, um, six or seven inches taller than me—" she emphasized the word *taller,* and ignored his eyes, sparkling with what she strongly suspected was laughter "—and outweighs me by probably fifty or sixty pounds. Yet, if I'd used full force against him, he'd be on the floor right now. And I wasn't even mad. When you add anger and fear to your strength, there's little you can't do, at least one-on-one.''

"Okay, let's recap," Tessa said two hours later. "What's the best way to get yourself out of trouble?"

"Practice," someone called out.

"How?"

"In your head, every day. And with your friends. It makes you be prepared for anything."

"Good. What's your best weapon?"

"Havin' you along, Miss Rose," Luis said.

"Your hands and feet," one of the girls said when the laughter died.

"Screaming," said another.

"Biting."

"All correct answers," Tessa said. "Make a lot of noise, fight as hard as you can and just as dirty."

"Don't believe anything your attacker tells you, 'cause he's lying," the quietest girl in the class said. She hadn't spoken during the entire two hours. "Get hurt fighting back, if you have to, instead of getting raped or—or worse."

"Exactly. Thanks for reminding us, Sherry."

"Don't ever let 'em take you somewhere. Crash the car, or make them crash it somehow," Luis added.

"Good. What's your primary goal?"

"To get away."

"Right. Everybody say that together, loud."

"To get away!" they yelled.

"Nobody tries to be a hero, right?"

"Right!"

"Mr. Ryan, do you want to add anything?" Tessa asked.

Chase approached the podium. "I think that at least once a month we should practice what we've learned today. And I say 'we' because I've been as much a student as you today. Miss Rose, that was an excellent program. I'm sure I speak for everyone when I say that we all feel more prepared. Thank you very much.''

She scooted the teenagers out of the room, embarrassed at the applause, happy to have everything she'd learned in the past twenty years or so be received with such enthusiasm.

''There's someone I'd like you to meet.'' Chase indicated the man standing, posture perfect, at the back of the room, as he had been for the two hours of the program.

She judged him to be in his seventies, although his solid body could have passed for a lot younger. His buzz-cut gray hair seemed perfect for his almost military demeanor.

''Tessa, this is Wilson Buckley, the man the Center is named for. Sarge, meet Tessa Rose.''

They shook hands. His was a firm handshake, not bone-crushing. Straightforward. Undoubtedly just like the man.

''I don't think I've been witness to a better program,'' Sarge said directly. ''You oughta take your show on the road. Run this at all the middle schools and high schools in the city.''

''We had a hard enough time getting some of the parents *here* to sign permission slips,'' Chase said. ''I had to call a lot of them personally. They live in denial of the dangers their children face today that they didn't.''

''With any luck,'' Tessa said, ''the kids will share their knowledge with their siblings and friends, maybe even their parents. Mr. Buckley, I'm really happy to meet you. Chase speaks so highly of you.''

''Call me Sarge.''

Chase excused himself to go change for dinner, leaving the two alone. They sat at a nearby table.

''How do you like working here?'' Sarge asked.

''It's the best job I've had, the best people I've worked with. You must be proud.''

''To have the Center named after me? Embarrassing, to tell you the truth. Seems like a person should be dead before they name something after 'em.''

Tessa smiled. "I think it's nice to be recognized while you can enjoy the notoriety."

"I couldn't talk Chase out of it." He rested his arms on the table and clasped his hands. "He's single-minded about most things."

"I've kind of noticed that about him. He works too hard, too."

"You thinkin' about changin' that, Miss Tessa Rose?"

The way he said her name made her pause. "You don't approve?"

He waited a few beats before he answered. "How is your family?"

Her heart rate escalated. "My family?"

"Yeah, family. Father, mother, brother..."

"You know them?"

"Used to know pretty much everybody hereabouts. Lost track of some."

"I see."

He leaned toward her. "I don't know what your motives are, but I'm tellin' you, don't you hurt that boy."

Tessa swallowed. "It's the last thing I want."

"I can see you're a decent person, Tessa Rose, and I don't think you'd want to hurt him. But you could and likely will. Whatever he did, he's paid for it. Long ago."

"I know."

"Do you?"

"I just wanted to meet him. Then when I met him, I wanted to know him. The more I know him, the more I like him." She leaned forward. "Are you going to tell him?"

Sarge pushed himself upright and stared hard at her. "That should come from you. But have a care, Miss Tessa Rose. Some people who seem strongest on the outside are the most fragile inside."

Tessa nodded, unable to utter a sound. She sat motionless until Chase rejoined her a little later.

"Sarge gone?" he asked.

"Yes."

He bent to capture her gaze. "Are you all right?"

She made herself smile as she stood. "I'm starving."

"Let's go, then."

Chase realized he was more aware of his surroundings than he'd ever been as they walked to the restaurant. It wouldn't be dark for a couple of hours yet, making it easier to be on the lookout for Stone Man, reminding Chase that Les hadn't gotten back to him with information on the teenager or on Dodger yet.

He let the thought go. The cool summer evening seemed made for holding hands and strolling. But strolling was a bad idea, according to Tessa's lecture, and he'd also promised himself no hand-holding. He was trying hard to remember why.

They walked several blocks without speaking. "Are you worn out?" he asked finally, curious about her silence.

"Kind of. The kids were great, though, weren't they? I loved the way the girls wouldn't let the boys joke about anything. As soon as the boys got as serious as the girls, they really accomplished a lot."

"It's a good group."

"Thanks to you."

"These kids weren't hopeless to start with. My goal has always been to hook them in before they get involved in things they shouldn't. And some of the best counselors we've had are gang members who've matured out of the gangs. They don't pull any punches when they describe what the life is really like. But kids who don't have much of a family life are the most vulnerable, because they're searching for a connection, and they'll settle for what they can get. We have to catch them at the right moment." They stopped at a traffic signal. He found himself eyeing the drivers as each car passed.

"Tell me about Sarge. How did you meet him?" she asked.

"I was assigned to his foster care."

"Why?"

The old hurts should have faded some by now, but they hadn't.

It didn't seem as if they ever would. "I never knew my father. My mother disappeared when I was fourteen. To this day I don't know what happened to her. I was made a ward of the court. Sarge had just retired from the force and decided to take me in, and then other boys through the years. But I was his first. We have almost a father and son bond, at least as much of one as I'll ever know."

"Is that why you started the Center?"

"How do you know I started it?"

"It's public record, Chase. I did a lot of research on the Center and you before I applied for the job. I had to know what I was getting into, especially since I would be supporting myself fully for the first time. I couldn't afford a job that might not be there in a few months."

When they settled at their table at the restaurant and had ordered drinks, he questioned her about being on her own for the first time.

"I was overprotected." She grimaced. "That's an understatement. I was smothered. And good daughter that I was, I didn't venture away from the family fold even when I went to college or when I got a full-time job. My brother is disabled, and my mother can't always cope with him. So it fell to me a lot."

"Why did you make the move now?"

The waitress set two bottles of beer and some chips and salsa on the table. Tessa took a long sip before she answered. If Sarge had figured her out already, how long until Chase did?

"They say women have their midlife crisis ten years earlier than men," she said. "That's the only explanation I can give without sounding extremely selfish. My brother needs to learn to help himself, but my mother doesn't see that. My parents argue about it quite a bit. Anyway, it's time to test my wings. It's hard to have a social life when your parents grill every guy, practically demanding proof of clean police, DMV and medical records."

"Social life," Chase mused. "Remind me of what that is."

She swirled a finger around the lip of the bottle as she tilted her head and smiled at him. "Interaction between man and woman. Movies. Meals. Conversation. Physical contact."

He reached across the table and took her hand, toying with her fingers before linking them with his and holding tight. "I had the best of intentions about tonight," he said, his voice gruff. "But no willpower."

"I'm so glad."

"I don't want to mislead you. My life—"

"Social contact, Chase. That's all this is. It's good for both of us."

He released her hand and sat back, eyeing her as he swigged his beer. "So, would your parents approve of me?"

*My parents would have me kidnapped and taken to a deprogrammer.*

"Are you ready to order?"

The waitress's intrusion sent the conversation in a different direction, and they didn't speak of personal history again. She'd been encouraged by the apparent laughter in his eyes earlier at the Center and so tried again, but couldn't tease the slightest smile out of him. Deciding not to push it, she settled back in her chair and relaxed, enjoying his observations on life, admiring the tough stand he took on an individual's accountability for his or her own actions. He lived in a black-and-white world—it was the only way he could function—while hers was much more gray, with room to change her opinion, given the right debate.

They stayed at the table for hours. The restaurant was obviously a favorite hangout of Chase's, as he seemed to know almost everyone there. Curious looks lit on her, but no one teased him or pried. They just welcomed her to their world, making her feel at home.

The ocean breezes nipped at them as they walked to her apartment later. Warmed by his hand wrapped around hers, she lifted her face to the wind and smiled as her hair blew behind her.

"Luis asked me that first day," he said, "if you were one of those Amazons he'd studied in school. I told him you weren't tall enough. But you do look like I've always suspected a Valkyrie would.''

"Weren't they women warriors, too, like the Amazons?"

"Not quite. They chose the warriors who were invited to die heroically in battle."

She flashed him a grin. "What tipped you off? My bloodthirsty cries?"

"You do have a powerful set of, uh, lungs."

"Why, Mr. Ryan. You're flirting with me! I'm flattered."

"You have wisdom, Tessa. And strength. That's why I think of you as a Valkyrie."

"Even though I could bring about a warrior's destruction?" The image planted itself in her mind and stayed. She didn't like it.

"I guess he'd die happy."

She squeezed his hand. "I thought *I* was supposed to be the idealist here, and you the pragmatist. If you get fanciful on me, I won't know how to deal with you."

"That suddenly holds appeal for me."

They entered the tiny lobby of her apartment house, the stairs directly in front of them. She turned around and climbed the steep steps backward, watching him, trying to read his expression as she clasped his hand tighter with each step up.

"You're going to trip on your skirt," Chase cautioned, tension creeping into him.

When she almost did trip, she let go of his hand, then scooped up the fabric and held it almost to her knees.

"So you do have legs. I've been wondering," he said.

"Have you?"

"Yeah. You never wear jeans?"

"Rarely. I like the feel of fabric drifting around me."

His imagination wandered on a sensual journey. When she reached the top of the stairway, and he stood three steps below her, he stopped her from moving on. He ran his free hand along her leg, starting at her ankle, gliding slowly to her knee. His gaze locked with hers. "Your skin is so soft. Like you, Tessa. Like all of you." He climbed the steps to join her on the landing. "I haven't had softness in my life."

She slid her arms around his waist as he framed her face with his hands. Her breasts rested against him. He closed his eyes for a second, savoring the contact, then pressed his lips to her temple, inhaling the clean, flowery fragrance of the curls tickling his nose. He bent closer still, threading his fingers through her hair, rubbing his cheek leisurely against the silken tresses, feeling her pull herself more snugly against him, a soft sigh escaping—

"Sorry, Tess. Just passing through."

They jumped apart at the interruption. Chase saw her struggle to focus on the man who waited on the stair below them, needing to get by.

"Um. Norm, hi. Please excuse us."

She took a step back, introducing the men at the same time. Chase followed her, leaving enough room for her neighbor to walk past. The man didn't hesitate to leave them alone, but the interruption brought about a return of Chase's earlier intention not to let this relationship get too serious.

When Norm shut his apartment door, Chase spoke to Tessa before she could invite him in.

"I'll see you Monday," he said, ignoring the disappointment in her eyes.

Her face was flushed a soft pink, either a remnant from their embrace, or embarrassment from being stumbled upon by her neighbor. It was a pretty face, one he wouldn't mind waking up to. He didn't think she could say the same about him. His early-morning face was probably safe for public viewing only on Halloween.

He brushed his fingertips along her cheek, tucked her hair behind her ear. "It was a nice evening. Thank you, Tessa. Now, please let me see you safely into your apartment."

She trapped his hand against her face and smiled, warming him clear through to his bones.

"I wouldn't want you to think I'm easy," she said. "After all, this is our first date." She raised her brows, as if daring him to deny another such momentous occasion would occur. "But I don't like not knowing what you would have done if Norm hadn't interrupted us."

"There's a saying, Tessa..."

"Yes?"

He took the keys she'd pulled from her skirt pocket, located one that seemed appropriate and opened her door, passing the key chain back to her as she glided by him. "Always leave 'em wanting more."

# Four

Chase regretted not kissing her good night.

He might have left her wanting more, but he'd denied himself, too, which distracted him all the next day. Even as a teenager, he'd had more control of his thoughts, his passion. He usually faced a dilemma head-on, but this one had blindsided him, and he couldn't seem to angle it down a straighter path. He was wishing for something he couldn't have, setting himself up for the biggest fall of his life.

Because Sunday was the only day of the week he allowed himself a long stretch of personal time, he took his distracted self to the local bookstore to wander, his favorite pastime. His gaze kept landing on books he'd hardly noticed before. He thumbed through a few, but didn't want to buy any because the clerk knew him, and this subject was far afield from his usual reading list.

Just how juvenile was that? he wondered, rubbing his forehead. Thirty-two years old and he was worried about someone thinking he might be interested in the opposite sex? Not that he hadn't been interested before, but his attention level had risen sharply, as if his knowing everything there was about women and how to please them was more critical than curing cancer.

Giving in to the urge that kept drawing him back to the Health and Psychology section, he chose a book and slid it behind his copy of *Beyond Ethnicity and Gender*. He headed toward the cashier, then ran right into Tessa coming from the children's section, her stack of books teetering for a second before she grabbed them tighter, preventing them from tumbling.

They said each other's name at the same time, then a long silence ensued. Finally she smiled, which not only meant that her mouth curved upward, but her whole face took on a radiant glow. Tessa Rose was deep-down, through-every-cell beautiful. The long, flowered dress she wore only added to her femininity, even as the modest neckline hid any hint of cleavage.

Although cradling the books in her arms, she pressed a palm to his chest, as though she couldn't stop herself. He covered that soft, warm hand with his, sliding it to rest against his heart, keeping it there. And then, because he seemed to have lost all ability to control his actions, he leaned over her pile of books and kissed her—more than a greeting, less than a seduction. He heard a tiny whimper rise in her throat and felt it vibrate against his lips. People brushed by them, no one saying anything. The wonder of San Francisco, he thought.

He lifted his head and looked at her as she opened her eyes slowly.

"Well," she said, her cheeks taking on a pink hue. "Good afternoon to you, too."

"That was good night. This is good afternoon." He wrapped his free arm around her, pulled her as snugly to him as the barrier of books allowed, and really kissed her, not caring who watched. What mattered most was the way her fingers clutched his shirt as her tongue met his, shyly, then with a boldness he wanted to explore but knew he couldn't. Not here, anyway. Not now.

"Mmm." Her heels lowered to the floor again as he moved

back. She blinked once, then again. "Um. You make up for lost opportunities very nicely."

"I've been kicking myself since I left you last night." The words poured out as if someone had turned on a spill-your-guts faucet. He didn't like it, but he couldn't seem to change it.

"Have you?" Her voice caught a little. "I've been kicking you, too. Metaphorically, that is."

He ran his fingertips over her eyebrow, along her temple, down her cheek. His thumb brushed her lips, still moist from their kiss, parting them. "I hardly slept," he said, letting his hand drift down her neck, then across her shoulder to skim along her arm, the downy hair rising in response.

"Me, neither."

He got pulled in by those baby blue eyes that made him wish his life had been different, normal. Even seminormal. He glanced at her books, but his eyes focused on her nipples, which pressed against the summer-weight fabric molding her full, high breasts. Primitive images flooded his mind, urgent cravings he not only couldn't control, but didn't want to. He slid his books in front of him.

"This is going really fast, Tessa."

"I'm as shocked as you are." She looked in the direction of the coffee bar. "Would you like to get something to drink? Or maybe you have to get back to the Center?"

"I have time." He realized they'd be at the cash register together paying for their books. Stalling, he looked at her stack again. "I see you've stocked up. What did you get?"

She tugged the books closer. Her cheeks turned a deeper pink. "Just some of my favorites."

Bewildered at her apparent embarrassment, he angled his head to look at the titles, but she tipped the spines down.

"I'll show you over coffee," she said. "What did you get?"

"Grisham, and this one." He let her see the top book.

"What else? You've got a third."

He waited until she looked up at him, curiosity in her eyes.

"A psychology book." He gestured toward the cashier. "After you."

"Um. You go ahead," she said. "I forgot something. I'll meet you." She hurried off.

Chase could see her reflection in the plate-glass window of the store. He decided to get rid of the copy he'd picked up of *Unspoken Pleasures: What women wish every man knew,* so that there was no chance she'd see it. He watched her glance furtively toward the front of the store, toward him. She angled down the Health and Psychology aisle, stopped for a second, then scurried along to the children's section.

Instead of sliding his book into one of the Hot New Fiction stacks close to the register, he returned to the Health and Psychology section, more than a little curious about what he might find. Sure enough, one book looked as if someone had tossed it there—*What Men Won't Tell You: How to recognize and satisfy a man's needs.*

He sought her with his gaze. She seemed in deep concentration as she stared at a bookshelf, but her hair had fallen over her shoulders, blocking his view of her face. So, they both were interested in improving their relationships with the opposite sex. And they both had chosen books meant to help them please the other person, not themselves.

Something warm threaded through him, slow and peaceful, tender and content. She'd chosen the book because of him. He didn't doubt it for a second. Deciding that no written word could give him more confidence, he returned his book to its place, then he moved near Tessa, taking her stack of books and adding them to his.

"I'm glad I ran into you," he said simply.

"Me, too."

Which was an understatement, Tessa decided, as they moved toward the cash register a minute later. She liked him. A lot. She liked that he was six feet tall and had broad shoulders and narrow hips and a flat abdomen. She liked his dark hair and stormy eyes.

She liked that his face was interesting, not handsome exactly, but appealing in a way she would never be able to describe adequately. Yet his appearance meant little when weighed against his intelligence and character.

And she loved that he surprised himself constantly with the things he said and did with her, especially kissing her in public as he had. She never would have expected it of him.

They lingered over coffee for so long that Tessa was going to be late for dinner at her parents' house unless she caught the next bus. She didn't want to leave him or their conversation, which jumped from personal to professional to philosophical and back to personal in a flash. Most of the time they held hands across the table, and she found herself wishing he'd invite her home, just to keep talking. And maybe a little something else.

She'd had a close call with the book. If he'd seen it, though, he might have invited her, and she wouldn't be sitting there all warm and aroused and sensitized just from the way his fingers twined with hers and his eyes caressed her. Maybe she should have let him see what she'd planned to buy instead of being worried what he might think of her.

Of course, if she'd picked up the one she'd really wanted to get, he might have thought something worse. The title had tempted her enough that she'd flipped through it, reading parts in great detail, trying to retain the ideas. Oh yes, *Multiple Orgasms: They're not just for women anymore* was chockful of creative suggestions she wouldn't mind testing.

But he didn't invite her home, and now she had to leave.

He walked her to the bus stop and kissed her goodbye as the bus pulled up, then waited until it was out of sight. As she watched him fade with distance, she wondered if he had hair on his chest. If he wore briefs or boxers. What his mouth would feel like on her breasts.

The attraction was more than a little dangerous. Was that part of his appeal? No. She didn't think so, anyway. He wasn't dangerous, just the attraction, because of the secret she guarded. The one that Sarge knew about. The one that could destroy what was growing between her and Chase. Time. She just needed time.

Her emotions were simmering, a warm, satisfying bubbling of happiness. Would it lead to a physical relationship? It seemed more than a possibility. And she wanted to be prepared when the time was right. Books could answer a lot of her questions. Although personal experience... She let her imagination drift with images.

The bus rumbled to a stop, and she got off. She could see her brother through the living room window, watching her approach. She waved and smiled as she started up the ramp that replaced the stairway to the house. He lifted a hand, which pleased her.

Maybe she'd been dreading the evening for no reason. Maybe her first visit home would be okay, after all. Already there was a change in her brother. Just the fact he'd waved meant something.

She'd moved out because she needed to break her role of caretaker, so now it was up to her to force changes. It would be good for all of them. She just had to make them see that.

And she would hug her blossoming relationship with Chase to herself for a while longer. No sense destroying bridges before they were even built.


Chase eased himself into a tub of hot water, sighing as the welcoming warmth soothed his aching body. His long-standing Sunday-night basketball game with his friends had taken more out of him than usual.

Gabe had brought along his woman-of-the-moment, and made efficient use of every opportunity to impress her with his athletic skills.

Ben seemed to be exorcising demons as he drove the ball hard down the court every time he got hold of it, never caring who he crashed into, as long as he made the basket. Chase had stopped counting how many times he'd ended up on his butt because Ben had shouldered him out of the way.

He missed Sebastian, who would have openly kidded Gabe

about showing off for the adoring woman, and then reminded Ben that this was supposed to be a game between friends. But Sebastian wasn't around these days, and the group's cohesiveness had disintegrated without him as the glue.

So, Chase, Gabe and Ben had played one-on-one-on-one, making their own rules, which seemed to be either Play Hard or Play To Impress or Play To Kill, depending on who had the ball.

Chase leaned his head back against the rim of the tub and closed his eyes. The men—and Les—had been friends since they were fourteen years old, but each was going through changes they weren't inclined to talk about.

The bath water cooled to room temperature before he roused himself to climb out of the tub. He swiped a towel along his body, flopped onto his bed and picked up a book from his nightstand. He wondered whether Tessa was home. If she'd bought that book today, would she be stretched out on her bed, too, reading?

His concentration shot, he pictured her lying naked on her bed, as he was, the warm-for-San Francisco evening allowing for windows to be open and the ocean breeze to cool the room. Putting his book aside, he rolled to his back and stared at the ceiling, recalling her eyes, her mouth, her breasts. The hard crests poking at her dress.

Her long hair would easily cover her breasts if she pulled it over her shoulders. Would she hide behind her hair? Would she mind being held close all night, or would she need her own space? He wanted to hold her. All night. Forev—

Chase pushed himself upright. He sat on the side of his bed for a few minutes, staring at the telephone. It was ten o'clock. Too late? She called herself a night owl, not a morning person.

He dragged the phone onto the bed. Dialed. Waited. One ring. Two—

"Hello?"

"Hi." He couldn't think of a single creative thing to say.

"Hi, yourself. I was hoping you'd call."

"How was your evening?"

"It was okay. Nobody argued. Even my brother was in good spirits. How was your basketball game?"

"Grueling." He told her about Gabe showing off and Ben being out to punish himself and therefore the others, for some unknown reason.

"Ben's the one who was married to your friend Leslie, the police detective, right?" she asked.

"Yeah. The idiot. How he could have divorced Les is beyond me. He was a fool to let her go."

And how could anyone believe in marriage when those two couldn't keep it together? That was something he and Gabe and Sebastian *had* talked about. Ben and Leslie were the most perfect couple they'd known. Their divorce had been hard on all of them.

"No one knows what goes on in a marriage except the two people involved, Chase. You may have known them forever, but you didn't live with them."

"Is that experience talking?" He hadn't considered that she'd been married. Jealousy slashed into him. He resented it.

"Not personal experience. I haven't been married, if that's what you're asking. How about you?"

"Not even close. It's hard to divide my time when the needs here at the Center are so overwhelming."

"Everyone needs a social life, though. I think you should put yourself in my hands," she said, then made a little sound he couldn't identify. "Um. I mean— Oh, shoot. Well." She blew out a breath. "Say something, please."

Images swirled around him, vivid and erotic. He wouldn't mind putting himself in her hands, of course, or putting her in his hands. Did he have the right? After all the years of self-denial, could he allow himself that freedom?

"Chase?"

"I'm here."

"I've been too forward, haven't I? I've made you uncomfortable. I know you're sort of my boss, but—"

"I'm not—either uncomfortable or your boss, so put that out of your mind completely."

"Okay." She paused. "I guess I'll say good night, then."

He said good night with a calmness he didn't feel. He'd have to slow things down. He didn't want her to assume they could have a future, especially a near future.

He'd never expected to make a commitment to a woman. He was still doing penance. That wasn't going to stop. Self-denial was the price he'd paid, willingly, all these years for what he'd done. The financial retribution he made monthly also helped him cope, but the continuing personal sacrifices were what eventually might bring him self-forgiveness.

It was too much to think about. He turned out the light instead, closed his eyes and drifted. Tomorrow would bring the same questions, the same dilemmas, but with a fresher perspective.

Chase wasn't in his office the next morning when Tessa arrived for work. Disappointed, she turned from his doorway and headed for the day care center, relaxing as she went—or as close to re-laxing as was possible. She wouldn't have believed that the hu-man body could sustain such tension for days on end without suffering in some way. Her appetite had dwindled and she no longer slept undisturbed. Her dreams were exciting and detailed, if exhausting. In them, Chase smiled back, because his past was erased. The link they shared was gone, as well, giving them both clean slates.

Dreams, indeed. Sometimes she forgot. Sometimes she thought they could have a normal relationship.

Over the next hour she watched for him, sure he'd drop by at some point, but the only person who came was Dodger. Pushing a handcart stacked with the food delivery, he called a cheerful hello, then went straight to the kitchen. She returned the greeting but paid him little attention. She and the children were painting, and the job required her full attention, or the chairs, walls and doors would become their canvases.

"Are you done?"

Startled by the fierce male voice, Tessa turned and saw Chase filling the doorway. His gaze wasn't on her, however, but on Dodger, who lounged against a wall.

"It's cool, man." He pushed the cart ahead of him as he crossed the room.

"Go to my office," Chase said.

"Okeydokey." The wheels clattered against the floor. "So long, Miss Rose. See you on Wednesday."

"Bye," she said, then turned her gaze on Chase.

"When you break for lunch, come to my office, please," he said.

Tension radiated from him. She wanted to put her arms around him, lay her head on his chest and hold him. Just hold him. "Sure."

"Thanks."

He was gone, leaving her more than a little curious. She counted off the minutes until she could take a break, then she grabbed her lunch bag and headed to his office. He wasn't sitting at his desk poring through paperwork, as usual, but standing with his back to the room, staring out the window.

She closed the door behind her, letting the noise announce her instead of words. She figured they shouldn't kiss hello here, and he was obviously in unspoken agreement. He waved off her offer to share her sandwich as he sat.

"What's wrong?" she asked finally, unable to bear the tension another minute.

"I spent the morning at the police station. I've worked with them for years, mostly counseling first-time offenders, teenage and younger. Because of it, and because of Sarge and Les, as well, I know a lot of cops. I've earned a position of trust there, and I've never violated it."

Of course he hadn't. The thought was absurd. "What happened?"

He pushed his fingers through his hair, then set his arms on his desk. "I asked Les to check out Dodger and Stone Man, the kid who tried to grab your purse."

"And you don't like what you learned."

"I can't give you specifics. Stone Man—his real name is Bobby Moran—has been brought in for questioning a couple of times, but they haven't been able to get anything to stick. I'd like to get my hands on him, because I'd like to see if we could help turn him around. He's fourteen. Too young for so many people to have given up on him. But although he's impressed the local kids with his daring, he hasn't gone big-time yet."

"So there's hope."

"Slim, but yes. I'm going to try to track him down. I wanted you to know my intentions so you won't be shocked if he shows up."

Tessa knew he was thinking of himself at fourteen, how someone had given him a chance. She picked up half her sandwich, then shoved the other half toward him. "Eat. You need it more than I do."

"I'll go up to my apartment when we're done."

"Eat or I'm leaving."

Resigned, Chase bit off the corner of the ham-and-cheese sandwich. Hungrier than he realized, he didn't speak again until he was finished. Then she set four peanut butter cookies in front of him.

"Okay, now you can talk," she said.

He broke a cookie in two and savored one half, letting her wait. She didn't seemed annoyed, though, instead rather pleased that she'd gotten her way. "It's about Dodger," he said at last. "If I had a choice, he'd never be allowed in here, but I don't, because he's employed by the food bank. From now on, though, he will come to my office first and I'll escort him to the kitchen. If he ever shows up without me, send an aide to get me right away."

"If you're so worried about him, why can't you ask the food bank to replace him?"

"Unless he breaks a law, I can't. I just don't want it to get that far." He wished he could tell her the details, but his hands were tied with legal twine. He could only caution her to be careful around him. She hadn't seen the way Dodger looked at her earlier. But Chase had. Added to what he knew, he was more than a little worried. "Don't ever be alone with him, Tessa. And if you see him single out one of the girls, intervene."

"I'm assuming the other teachers are being told the same thing?" She challenged him with her eyes.

Prickly. He liked that. She wanted to be sure she wasn't being treated differently because of the personal relationship growing between them. "All of the adult workers will be told."

"Good." She split a bunch of grapes and tossed half to him.

"I do remember to eat, Miss Rose." He popped a grape in his mouth as he watched her do the same, only she tossed hers high in the air and caught it in her mouth. With a wicked grin she arced one his way. He angled to his left. It bounced off his nose.

Because she laughed, he lobbed one back at her, which she caught neatly.

"Ha!" she said, implying more.

"Mine was a better toss."

She stopped chewing. Her eyes lit with humor. "Oooh, and a manly ego, too."

"It's the truth. Your aim stunk."

"Stunk? *Stunk?* Why, Chase Ryan, I'll have you know I was an all-state guard on the varsity girl's basketball team in high school. I still hold the record for scoring, in a single game *and* a season."

"Now whose ego needs stroking?"

She flew out of her chair and rounded his desk, her hair bouncing, her breasts—

Chase swallowed. They were right in front of his face. He could reach out and touch. Reluctantly he lifted his gaze. She bent toward him. Lightning zapped through him in anticipation as she rested her hands on the padded arms of his chair. Her hair drifted over her shoulders and brushed his forearms. His body went on full alert.

"It's not my *ego* that needs stroking," she whispered, the tiniest smile on her face, one that disappeared as she got closer, then her lips touched his.

He dragged her into his lap, bent her over and devoured her mouth. Never mind that his office was no place to kiss her. Never mind that his door was unlocked. Never mind that he got hard with need so fast it hurt. This was Tessa. Soft and fragrant and giving. How she could excite and comfort him at the same time was a wonder, but she did.

He slid his hand from the small of her back to her waist, a slow glide of pleasure. Her skin was warm through her blouse—and her body distinctly female. He inched higher, until he encountered the band of her bra. She drew a quick, sharp breath, then backed away a little and looked at him, her eyes dark and glittery, as he felt her breast rest heavily, beautifully, against his thumb. She moaned and closed her eyes. Her lips parted. He fanned his hand over her breast, felt her hard nipple burn his palm, even through the double layer of fabric.

She made a kind of whimpering sound before she slammed her mouth, open and hot, against his, giving and taking. Demanding.

He needed to feel her skin, needed to know if she was as soft as he'd imagined. He tugged her blouse free of her skirt, encountering the body so temptingly different from his. She breathed his name against his lips, going perfectly still as he skimmed his hand under her bra, wishing he could just tear it off her, wishing he could know what her nipple felt like against his tongue.

She arched her back, hinting at her own needs. He lifted his head, staring at her as he moved a hand to her thighs, her skirt having pooled around her hips when he'd tipped her back. He watched her face as he pushed the fabric a little higher. Her eyelids lowered, but she didn't shut her eyes. He trailed his fingertips along her thigh until he encountered fabric. Soft, silky, damp fabric. She moaned as he touched her there. At her involuntary sound, he almost lost control of himself. He slipped a finger under the elastic edge—

A loud knock sounded. Tessa scrambled off his lap, apologizing when he made a pained sound. Her skirt was twisted and tangled so that she couldn't take a step until she shook it into place.

Another knock, even louder.

She jammed her blouse into her waistband.

"Chase?"

"It's Ben," Chase said, starting to stand, then realizing he couldn't, not without Ben seeing—

The door opened.

"Chase?"

Tessa felt her face burn with embarrassment, the heat radiating down her body until even her feet sweat. She didn't dare look at Chase, but the tightness in his voice indicated a similar reaction in him.

"Ben. Come on in."

"Why didn't you answer? Oh." His gaze landed on Tessa. He seemed to make a quick and accurate assessment of what he'd interrupted. A slow smile stretched across his lips as he drew near, extending his hand to her. "Ben O'Keefe."

"Tessa Rose," she said, warming to his smile. He was bigger than Chase but he didn't have the hard edges that made Chase's face so compelling, the edges that reflected his character so wonderfully.

"The new preschool teacher," Chase added.

"I see." Ben paused a few beats. "If this is a bad time—"

"Actually," Tessa announced as she moved to pick up her lunch remains, "I was just leaving. It was very nice meeting you."

"Same here."

Chase watched her hurry out and pull the door shut behind her with a whoosh, sending a breeze through the room. He dared Ben with his eyes. "She *is* the new teacher."

Ben's brows lifted. He took the seat across the desk. "You don't lie. Everyone knows that."

Chase relaxed. He'd known Ben for too long to worry about his reaction. They kept each other's secrets, he and Ben and Gabe and Sebastian. And Leslie. He could tell Ben about Tessa. He just didn't have everything sorted out yet.

"I came to apologize for last night," Ben said. "I was rough on you and Gabe. Something happened...and I took it out on you."

Chase nodded—an acceptance of the apology but an unspoken invitation, as well, if Ben wanted to talk.

Ben pushed himself out of the chair. He wandered to a bookcase and stared at the titles there. "It's Les, of course."

"I saw her this morning. She didn't say anything."

"That's the worst of it. There's nothing to say, I guess." He turned back around, shoving his hands in his pockets. "I ran into her Saturday night. With her date. It was the first time... Damn it—" He stopped. "I'm sorry."

"The kids can't swear here, Ben. You're not breaking any rules."

"Yeah, okay." He returned to plop into the chair again. "I'd never seen her with anyone else, you know? It was hard. I know I have no right."

"That's true."

Ben frowned. "It's been over two years. I shouldn't feel this way."

"You were together since you were fourteen. It's not going to die fast."

"That's not it. Not entirely. I know I couldn't stay in the relationship. It was killing me, day by day. But I've gotten on with my life. So, why won't I let her get on with hers?"

Chase had an opinion on that, but he didn't think Ben wanted to hear it. Once again, the question struck him: if Ben and Leslie couldn't keep it together, who could?

"Never mind. Rhetorical question," Ben said, then blew out a breath. "I really did come here to apologize."

"Which I accept, provided you let me use your whirlpool later on today. You had me using muscles I didn't know I had."

Ben grinned. "Name the time, and I'll send the hotel masseur up to the suite afterward. It's the least I can do."

"I won't turn down that offer. Thanks."

He shrugged, then stood. "I'm sorry I interrupted your lunch—or whatever."

Chase followed him to the door, deciding he should be grateful it was just Ben who interrupted, not someone from the Center. "No problem."

"Uh-huh." His hand on the doorknob, Ben hesitated. "Thanks for listening."

"I'll always listen. You know that."

"And refrain from much comment. You know, if I'd talked to Sebastian like that about Les, he would have acknowledged my right to be jealous, then asked how I thought Les felt when she knew I'd been on a date."

"Yeah, and if it were Gabe, you would have listened to a five-minute lecture on how stupid you were for divorcing Les in the first place. You came to me for a reason, Ben."

Chase left the door open after Ben left, hoping someone else would come in and keep him from thinking about Tessa. How easy she was to talk to. How soft she felt, how wonderful she smelled, how good she tasted. There was so much he wanted to do to her. With her. For her.

When the fantasies started to overwhelm, he decided to hit the streets and see if he could spot Bobby Moran, the notorious Stone Man.

After an hour he found the boy, leaning against a signpost. His baggy pants and shirt needed a wash, his sneakers were brand-new and expensive, his hair long and amateurishly cut.

He reminded Chase of himself at the same age, except for the expensive shoes. Something twisted up inside of him, something he wished he could forget, but never could.

"Bobby Moran?" he asked when he reached the boy's side.

"Who wants to know?"

# Five

Five-fifteen in the morning was not a fit hour for woman or beast, Tessa thought as she yanked her shower curtain open and stepped dripping wet from the tub. One of the early-shift teachers had called ten minutes ago, begging Tessa to trade shifts today because her son was sick. What was Tessa supposed to say? I'm sorry, but I don't wake up before eight o'clock. Ever.

Of course not. Her mind may not be functioning at full speed but her body could do what it needed to.

Shivering, she dried herself off, then let her hair out of the knot she'd fashioned because there wasn't time to shampoo. She pulled on the skirt and blouse she'd laid out the night before, tied on her sneakers, brushed mascara on her lashes so that she looked somewhat awake. Into a lunch bag went fruit and trail mix. She figured Chase owed her a sandwich, anyway. Maybe she could even get herself invited to his apartment upstairs.

She smiled, liking the idea more as she considered it.

While shoving down a piece of toast, she filled a thermos with iced tea, then she forced her eyes to stay open as she brushed her teeth. Finally, she threw a sweater over her shoulders to ward off the morning and left the cocoon of her apartment.

Happiness settled over her as she headed for the Center. The kiss she'd shared with Chase yesterday in his office still lingered, probably because his phone call late last night was full of pregnant pauses, as if silently reminding her of the momentous event that had seemed to last a lifetime but was over in a flash.

She closed her eyes and drew a deep breath. The air braced her like a vitamin-rich tonic. In different circumstances she'd be grumbling all the way to work, given the time of day, but she was so anxious to see Chase that it didn't matter. Everything looked beautiful—the sidewalks, the houses, the storefronts, even the bus stops. Walking to work at five forty-five was a vastly different experience from ten forty-five, in sight and sound, even smell.

Absorbed in the new environment, she turned down a side street to take a shortcut to the Center. Two blocks to go. Two blocks until she saw him. Would they be alone long enough to greet each other in private? Or were people waiting for the doors to open? Would she beat Chandra there? She slid her hand into her skirt pocket and wrapped her fingers around her keys. One block left. She pictured his face—smiling. Sometime, somehow, she was going to make that happen, even if it—

Footsteps pounded behind her. Close. Too close. She hadn't been paying attention. She clenched the keys tighter as she started to turn. Someone hit her full force with a running tackle. Asphalt scraped her cheek like hot coals. Stars burst in her eyes, blindingly brilliant. Then blackness sucked her into a cold, hollow, endless tunnel.

Chase dried his face and hands, hung his bath towel over the shower curtain rod, then slipped into a freshly ironed chambray shirt. He'd roll up the sleeves as the day warmed, but for now the cold seeped into his skin, sending a chill clear through. He tucked his shirt into his jeans and headed for the kitchen. A bowl of cereal would suffice until lunch.

He carried the full bowl into the living room, eating as he walked. Glancing around the room, he wondered what Tessa would think. That he lived like a monk? She'd be right. A complete remodeling had been budgeted into this year's allocations, but that job was on hold until—if—Sebastian returned.

Could a woman be content here? There wasn't a view to speak of, and the neighborhood wasn't the world's best, but when the remodeling was complete, the kitchen would be doubled in size and another bedroom added, as well as the bathroom modernized and some larger windows installed in the living room, with something other than basic blinds covering them.

Still, there wasn't a picket fence in sight. And no room for a garden. Street sounds penetrated the walls—buses, car alarms, sirens. He'd gotten used to the noise, could filter out what was normal from what wasn't.

Like that sound. What was that?

He stood still, listening. His name? Someone was calling his name and pounding on the outside door downstairs.

It sounded like—

Cereal and milk sloshed out of the bowl as he dropped it onto the coffee table. He ran across the room, yanked open the door, descended the stairs in four leaps. Her voice came up the stairwell with frightening clarity, words punctuated with pummeling, the metal door shaking with the force.

"Chase! Are you there? Oh, please be there. Chase! Oh, thank God!"

He had only a second to assess her condition—torn clothes, bloody face, wild eyes—then she pulled the door shut and leaned her forehead against it, grasping the knob with both hands.

"Tessa." He wasn't even sure he'd said her name aloud. He didn't know if he should touch her. His shock faded, only to be replaced by horror and fury and a multitude of emotions he couldn't take the time to sort out. "What happened? Let me see."

Her shoulders heaved as she gulped in air, but she turned around. Her face was scraped all down one side, her clothes ripped here and there and streaked with dirt. She flinched when he gripped her arms. He loosened his hold but didn't let go.

"I'm all right," she said between breaths. "The police. He's got...my bag."

"Who did this?" He'd kill him. Whoever did this, he'd kill him.

"Stay calm...please."

"Do you know him? What does he look like? Where did—".

"I need you here...with me," she interrupted. "Please, Chase. The...police?"

The violent red haze cleared. His place was with her, not chasing whoever had done this to her. "I won't leave you." He glanced at her arms and saw tiny asphalt pebbles embedded in her flesh. "Did he—?"

His jaw froze shut. The words wouldn't come. He struggled against an old image, as vivid as the day it happened. *Not Tessa. Please, not Tessa, too.*

She put a hand to her throat. "I fought him...off. Can we...go upstairs, please? My legs are pretty sh-shaky."

He started to lift her into his arms, but she stopped him.

"I want to walk. I hurt...everywhere."

Chase wrapped an afghan around her when he settled her on his sofa. Eighteen years of friendship gave him the right to contact Leslie at home. She said she'd call it in, then head over. He let Chandra know that she'd have to hold down the fort, and that she could pull in another teacher or a couple more aides.

All the while he watched Tessa. She burrowed into the afghan. A shiver passed through her, then she took a deep, settling breath. Her lips moved, as if she was talking to herself. He sat beside her and wrapped his hand around hers, finding more pebbles in her palm.

"I'm okay," she said, staring at her hand as he brushed her

palm gently, dislodging the grit. "I'm okay," she repeated with more force.

"Talk to me, Tessa."

She shook her head. She rocked.

He drew her to him carefully, offering comfort, resting his cheek on her curls. He stroked her hair, finding street debris there, too. She didn't relax in his arms but stayed taut, and was oddly fragile in her resistance.

They didn't move until two officers came, followed in a few minutes by police inspector Leslie O'Keefe.

Tessa watched the tall, auburn-haired woman approach, her eyes assessing Tessa as she neared. As soon as they determined where the crime occurred, Leslie sent the officers to investigate the scene, look for Tessa's purse and sweater and question potential witnesses.

Chase paced the room like a penned lion, back and forth, back and forth. Tessa tried to keep her gaze on Leslie, whose voice soothed as she drew out necessary information for her report.

"So he tackled you from behind and knocked you to the ground. You were unconscious, then?" Leslie asked, her pen poised on a small pad of paper.

"I think I came to right away. My bag was trapped under me. He shoved me, trying to get to it."

A harsh sound came from across the room. Tessa didn't look his way. She watched Leslie's eyes. She needed the quiet strength she saw there.

"Then what happened?"

Tessa tossed her hair back. "I screamed as loud as I could. He grabbed my purse and yanked. It made me fall onto my back. Then he leaned over me and I gouged his eyes and screamed again. He turned me loose."

"Can you describe him?"

"He wore a ski mask."

"Did you recognize his voice?"

She shook her head. "He didn't speak, except to shout when I poked his eyes. And he smelled funny."

"How?"

"Musty? I don't know. Nothing I recognized."

"But you'd recognize it again?"

"I don't think I could forget it." She finally glanced at Chase. He was leaning against a wall, his arms folded across his chest. His eyes— Well, his eyes were hard and dangerous and determined.

"What else can you tell me about him?"

Her head throbbing, Tessa pressed her fingers to her temples. "He wasn't as tall or muscular as Chase. He wore blue jeans and a white T-shirt that had something written on it, a music group, I think. I'll know it when I see it." She looked at Leslie then. "There was a tear in the right sleeve about the size of a quarter. He wore a watch with a black plastic band. Um, it had a buckle. I remember because it scraped my neck—" she turned her head for Leslie to see "—and it stung."

"Which wrist did he wear the watch on?"

She had to think about that. "The left. No rings. He was Caucasian."

Tessa's gaze flickered to Chase. She'd never seen a fiercer looking man in her life, nor one wound so tight.

"Do you think he was only after your purse?" Leslie asked. "When he leaned over you, was he still just trying to grab it away from you?"

Tessa stared at her. "Do you mean, was he going to rape me?"

Chase didn't move, but fury seemed to pour from him like lava, hot and unstoppable.

She turned her attention back to the inspector. "I don't know. I don't think so, though. I would've let him take the bag, Leslie." She rubbed her forehead. "I just wanted to get away, so I started running the second I got the chance. I don't know what he took. I think he was running in the other direction."

"You did the right thing. Now, who do you think might want to hurt you?"

"I can't imagine. I'm new here."

Leslie tapped her pen on her pad of paper. "Given that you weren't taking your usual route, and you normally arrive five hours later, my guess is this was a crime of opportunity. He saw you, decided—"

"No." Chase crouched on the other side of the coffee table. He looked at Tessa, but his words were for Leslie. "You checked them out yourself, Les. The kid, Bobby Moran, and Dodger. Physically, they fit the description."

"Motive?"

"Bobby was humiliated. I talked to him yesterday, tried to reach out. He ripped up my card and spat at my feet. Said 'the lady wouldn't be so lucky the next time.' And I read Dodger's rap sheet."

"But it wasn't her routine. It looks random, Chase."

"You'll check it out."

"Of course I will." She touched Tessa's face, turning her head, checking her injuries. "Your wounds need to be treated. Do you have a doctor?"

"Yes."

"See that it's taken care of right away. Asphalt burns are brutal. They take some deep cleaning."

Exhausted from holding in her feelings, Tessa just nodded.

"Here's my card," Leslie said. "You can reach my pager twenty-four hours a day. Call me if you remember anything else, or if you have any questions."

"It was just a mugging," Tessa said. "A simple mugging."

"I'm inclined to agree. But Chase isn't going to let me close the case until I know that for sure."

Chase glowered at Leslie, who smiled in return, not the least intimidated. Tessa was suddenly and profoundly grateful for Leslie's presence, and her longtime friendship with him. If there was the slightest chance the attack had been personal, Tessa wanted to know.

Chase followed Leslie out the door and down the stairs.

"Before you go back to her," she said, "we need to talk."

"About what?"

"Why didn't you tell me you met with the kid? Especially since he threatened Tessa."

"It just happened yesterday, Les. I would've called you today."

She eyed him steadily. "I've known you for a very long time. And I *know* you want to deal with this yourself."

He didn't deny it.

"I'm telling you to leave the police work to me. Not asking, Chase. Telling. Ordering. That's one strong woman in there. She provided a lot of information, more than the average victim. And I promise I'll stay on this myself. But you have to let us do our jobs."

"I'll give you a head start."

She hugged him. He gave in to the sympathy for a few seconds, holding her tight, then releasing her and shoving his hands in his pockets. "Find him, Les. Before I do."

"Let the legal system work, Chase. For now, make sure she gets her wounds treated. Does she have family she can go to?"

"I'll take care of her."

Leslie's brows lifted. "I see. I thought there was something... All right, then. I can reach you at her number today—or yours?"

"Either."

Just then the officers returned, reporting no sign of her purse or sweater. No one in the vicinity had seen or heard anything— or so they said.

Chase locked the door when they left. He found Tessa standing at the kitchen sink washing her hands and reported what the officers said. She continued to lather her hands.

"I'm going to drive you to the doctor."

"No."

He leaned a hip against the counter so he could see her face but her hair made a curtain he couldn't see through. "Les said—"

"I heard her. I just want to go home. I'll get myself clean."

"But—"

She turned toward him so fast he flinched. Her lips thinned to a hard line. Her eyes narrowed, hiding a glittery sheen that he didn't think was tears. She looked...fierce. Invincible. Angry.

Angry? *He* was angry. He didn't know what kind of emotion he'd expected from her, but not that. He forgot that she was strong and independent, because she seemed so soft most of the time.

"My grandmother knit me that sweater just before she died."

Ah. Now he understood. He laid his hand against her shoulder. "I'll go back myself and look for it, Tessa. I'll check trash cans. I'll put the word out."

Her gaze relaxed a little. She nodded, then turned her attention to her hands. "I have to go home."

Chase turned off the faucets. He took her hands in his, saw how raw they were. "I'll take you."

"Thank you," she said quietly. "Call Chandra and tell her I'll be back in a little while."

"You don't—"

"Yes, I do, Chase. I do."

"All right." He pulled two clean dishtowels from a drawer and wrapped one around each hand. "Sit down for a minute. I'll go talk to Chandra, and I'll also pick up some antiseptic from the first aid cabinet."

Tessa watched him go. When the door shut, she almost crumbled. She'd held her anger in check for so long that she was ready to explode from it. How could she have been so stupid? How? She'd been trained almost all her life to be on the alert. Then the one time she let down her guard she was caught. One time!

She paced his living room. If she hadn't been daydreaming about Chase, she wouldn't have forgotten to look around, to listen. But, oh, no. Her heart had been fluttering from her first step outdoors, and her hormones had added to it by remembering the kiss—and more—from yesterday.

And she couldn't tell him. He probably thought she was scared. She couldn't tell him the truth or he'd feel responsible. Guilty. He had enough guilt to deal with. It wasn't his fault that she'd been mooning over him like some teenager.

She had to relax. She had to let him know she was okay.

She prowled the room, her pace picking up. She also had to deal with her anger.

Hearing him hurrying up the stairs, she drew a deep breath. She could smile at him. She could let him know she wasn't some Pollyanna who didn't know what the real world was like. She knew, all right.

Now she had to convince him.

Chase called out his cavalry. Ben and Gabe met him where the mugging occurred, and they spent half an hour combing the area, looking for her sweater and purse, talking to people. They'd all grown up here. Ben and Gabe had moved on, but their ties were still strong. They knew how to ask questions, knew the unspoken code of silence that some neighborhoods could maintain. No one admitted to witnessing the event.

"Considering she screamed twice and he shouted once, I find it hard to believe that it went completely unnoticed," Chase said as they linked up to share their findings.

"It was too early for any of the businesses to be open," Gabe said. "There were only a couple of real possibilities for witnesses from residents."

"I know." Chase ran a hand through his hair. "I'll have to canvas later, when people get home, see if anyone heard anything on their way to work."

"Les'll have your head if you interfere," Ben said. "You know how she can get."

Gabe growled, showing his teeth. Ben smiled.

Chase glanced at his watch. "I've got to get back to Tessa's apartment. I told her I'd pick her up and take her to the Center. She should be done cleaning up by now.''

A car pulled up alongside the men. Leslie. She left the motor running, but climbed out of the car and approached them. Ben crossed his arms. Gabe grinned. Chase studied her, gauging the depth of her irritation, deciding she'd gone past irritated and on to irate.

''If it isn't the three musketeers.'' She fired the first salvo at Chase. ''I told you to stay out of this.'' Then she turned on Gabe. ''Wipe that smile off your face, mister.''

He laughed.

She touched a finger to his thigh. ''Got a smudge on your perfect linen pants, Gabriel.''

He looked down, missing the flicker of a smile that crossed her lips. Chase would tell him later.

''And you—'' she rounded on Ben ''—you were supposed to pick up our daughter fifteen minutes ago.''

''Oh, hell.'' He fished his car keys from his pocket. ''Call me later, Chase.''

Gabe made a quick exit, as well.

''Don't interfere,'' Leslie said to Chase when they were alone. ''I mean it. You called *me*. You put me in charge by doing that. Now back off and let me work.''

''I've got to go,'' he said, leaving her sputtering. Shifting mental gears, he wondered what kind of mood he'd find Tessa in. An improved one, he hoped, from the swings between forced cheerfulness and fury. Not that he hadn't been fascinated by each and every mood. He had.

Soft. Gentle. Strong. Determined. All the words applied. He couldn't wait to see which would greet him.

# Six

**T**essa flung the shampoo bottle against the tile. It ricocheted and landed on her foot, hard. The same foot she'd dropped the bar of soap onto three times already. She screeched.

She couldn't remember being so frustrated, so irritated, so angry.

"You all right in there?" a muffled male voice asked through the bathroom door.

Chase was back. He could help. No, he couldn't. Yes. No. She didn't know what to do.

She steadied herself with a slow breath. "Could you come in here?"

After a few seconds the door clicked open.

"You okay?" he asked, the sound of his voice indicating he'd just stuck his head into the room.

"No."

A long pause. "What's wrong?"

"I can't shampoo my hair. My hands are too scraped up. The shampoo stings like crazy and I can't rub the lather in."

Only the sound of the shower answered her.

"Could you help me, please?" she asked.

"How?"

"Would you shampoo me?"

A longer pause than before. "At the kitchen sink?"

"It has to be in the shower. My hair's too long to rinse in the sink." She waited for an answer. None came. "I can wrap a towel around me."

A towel was thrust behind the shower curtain. She smiled as she wound it around her and tucked a corner between her breasts. A minute later, he stepped in with her, wearing only jeans. All her anger and irritation disappeared. Her mouth went dry.

Distracted by his chest, which was broader than she'd imagined, she didn't say anything for a minute. "Thank you."

"Let me see your hands."

He inspected her palms, her arms, her neck, her face. "Looks like you got the dirt out okay. Anyplace else?"

"Shins."

He hesitated, then he crouched. She lifted one leg, then the other. Water fell over his head and shoulders.

He grabbed the shampoo from the bottom of the tub before he stood. "Looks good. Turn around."

Tessa luxuriated in his touch as he shampooed her hair, not saying a word, not touching her beyond what was necessary for the task. It took a long time to rinse. She turned off the water, then had him apply a conditioner and comb it through her hair.

He remained silent. She kept her back to him, but she was aware of every breath he took. Tension radiated from him.

He took his time untangling the curls. "I didn't find your purse or sweater, Tessa. I'm sorry. Gabe and Ben helped, too. There was nothing."

"It's okay."

"Do you have credit cards to cancel? Anything else of value?"

"Just my driver's license. I don't carry much. An art project for the children. My keys were in my pocket." She shivered, cold from the wet towel wrapped around her, and excited by his nearness.

"All done," he said finally, setting the comb aside. "Do you need anything else?"

"No. Thank you."

"I've got a change of clothes in my van. I'll be back in a minute." He stepped out of the tub, grabbed a towel and dried off. "Can you manage now?"

She nodded.

He watched her intently. "Are you sure?"

*Go on, ask him.* It wasn't as if he'd never seen a naked woman, after all. Just because she hadn't been naked in front of a man before—

"Tell me what you need, Tessa."

"Nothing. I'm fine. Really." It wasn't the truth. She knew how painful it was going to be to dry herself off and to dress. But she didn't see any alternative aside from asking him to help. She wouldn't do that.

So she watched him leave, then she sighed, knowing she'd just missed an opportunity she would probably regret.


"I'm spending the night," Chase said when he brought her home that night. "Whoever took your purse has your address. I won't leave you here alone."

"Okay."

"I'd feel better, at least for tonight," he said, shoving his hands in his back pockets. He didn't trust himself alone with her. He just didn't see any choice in the matter. She'd told him once today that she absolutely would not go to her family. She'd worked too hard for her independence to take that step back. That left *him.* "If you've got extra sheets, I'll fix a bed on the floor, using the sofa cushions."

"I said okay. Why are you being so belligerent?"

"No one's ever called me belligerent."

"Hostile?" she offered, the beginnings of a smile forming.

"Are you as recovered as you seem?" he asked abruptly. She'd gone about her workday as if nothing out of the ordinary had happened. She told the younger children she'd been in a little accident. The older ones knew the truth and were upset about it. She'd smiled and said everything was fine, adding that it was her inattention that had made her vulnerable, and reminding them to stay alert.

"Recovered? Probably not," she said. "But I don't see how worrying about it will help. It's done. I survived."

"I wonder if I will ever figure you out."

She smiled. That lethal smile he'd noted the first time he'd seen her. Why had his comment pleased her so much?

They made up a bed for him on the floor, then she went into the bathroom and shut the door. When she emerged a while later, she was wearing a knee-length, sleeveless nightgown, one that wasn't the slightest bit transparent, but that poleaxed him because he could see her breasts sway and the hard peaks press invitingly against the fabric.

He stalked into the bathroom, hoping that she'd be safely under covers by the time he came out. She wasn't. The lights were out, but she stood by her window looking out at the night. No moonlight illuminated the room, just a street lamp nearby that cast a bluish glow to her skin, making her seem pale and fragile. Needing protection. Needing him.

He stayed a distance from her.

"The world looks deceptively innocent from here, doesn't it?" she asked.

Because he couldn't comment without moving beside her, he took the ten steps necessary to do so.

"It's just a neighborhood, like many neighborhoods," she said. "Filled with different kinds of people, most of them good, hard-working men and women who only want to live in peace, raise their children, feel that they can walk their street safely. It looks so normal. Calm. Even welcoming. But that's an illusion, isn't it? We're never safe. Not anywhere."

"You're safe with me, Tessa."

"Am I?" she asked, turning to him and resting her hand against his chest, over his heart. "In what way? Safe from someone who meant me harm? Maybe. But not safe from the attraction I think we both feel. Not safe at all."

He pressed a hand to hers, then brushed gentle fingertips down her uninjured cheek. "Do you need to be safe from me?" He toyed with the button at her neckline. It popped open. So did the next. And the next. One more. The last one. His gaze never leaving hers, he slid his hand under the fabric, traced the slope of her breast, treasured her womanliness, welcomed the feel of her taut nipple in his palm.

Her lips parted. She made a soft, pleading kind of sound, and he bent closer, until his lips barely touched hers.

Tessa sighed, drawing up on tiptoe as he set his mouth on hers with such tenderness that tears sprang to her eyes. He breathed her name between gentle, healing kisses. She felt her nightgown slide down one shoulder, knew the moment her breast was bared to him. She let her head fall back as he traced a warm, wet path with his tongue, down her throat to the sensitive hollow between her breasts. One of his hands lifted her swelling flesh as his tongue swept her nipple, then his mouth settled there and his long groan vibrated against her flesh.

He pulled back without warning, dragged her close and held her fiercely, his lips pressed to her temple as he spoke, the words low and gruff.

"You can't imagine how I felt when I opened the door to you this morning. Fear. Rage. *Fury.* It unleashed something violent inside me that I didn't know was there."

Nothing had ever felt as good as being held in his arms. Good and cleansing and life-affirming.

"How did my world change overnight?" he asked, sounding bewildered.

*Destiny.* She couldn't tell him that without explaining everything, and the time for that wasn't right yet, so she burrowed closer. His chest was solid and warm beneath her cheek. The powerful muscles of his back bunched when she slid her hands from his waist up to his shoulder blades, then down again. She wrapped her arms around him.

"I want you, Tessa."

Her heart skipped more than a beat. Breathing took a conscious effort.

"But it wouldn't be right," he continued. "Not tonight. Not after what you've been through today."

She could feel his hard masculine need pressed to her abdomen, so she knew he was exchanging his own desire for her peace of mind. "I'm sure that someday I'm going to thank you for that, Chase. Someday." She leaned back and smiled. "Just not now. I'm sure you understand."

She tried to convince him to share the bed, but he wouldn't— which didn't surprise her. The last thing she remembered was the sound of him undressing in the darkness, followed by the rustle of sheets, then the most peaceful silence she'd ever known.

The night noises were new and strange. Chase lay with his arms crossed behind his head listening to her neighborhood, her apartment, *her*. She made sleepy sounds—sighs and murmurs. A whimper. A silky moan. She used the entire bed, tossing and turning, never staying in one position for long. She didn't seem to be having nightmares, just a restless night.

As was he, which was why he heard someone creep up the stairway of the apartment building and tiptoe to her door. Chase grabbed his jeans and hopped into them, not bothering to button the fly. He flung open her door and caught a glimpse of someone running, then disappearing down the stairs. He followed, but by the time he reached the sidewalk, no one was in sight. A fire engine approached, siren blaring, which blasted away any chance of hearing which direction the person had fled.

Chase retraced his steps, looking for clues. When he reached her door, he saw what he hadn't seen before—her Mary Poppins bag, which they'd assumed was gone forever.

Tessa came to the door just as he picked up her bag. She'd slid into her bathrobe. Across the hall, another door opened. Norm stuck his head out. He squinted at them, rubbing his eyes.

"What's going on?" he asked.

"Tessa was assaulted on her way to work today," Chase said coldly. "Someone just returned the purse she thought stolen."

"Assaulted? Are you all right, Tess?"

"Yes, thank you, Norm. He hurt my pride more than anything."

Chase hustled her back into the apartment after a terse farewell to her neighbor. He turned both of her locks, then switched on the light.

"Because the bag is fabric," he said, "the police can't lift any prints from it, but maybe from your wallet, or something else inside. We shouldn't touch anything."

"Can I just look inside?" She tilted the bag one way, then the other. "I don't think anything's missing. I can see my wallet."

They eased the wallet out with a pencil, then used two pencils to open it.

"The money's gone, but my driver's license is there. I'm just grateful he didn't get my keys, too."

"That's a good habit, keeping them in your pocket. How much money did you have?"

"About twenty dollars. Why would he return my bag? Why not just toss it in a dumpster?"

"We'll ask him. I'm pretty sure it was Bobby Moran, Tessa. I only got a quick look from behind, so I couldn't testify to it, but I'm almost positive."

"If he's the one who attacked me, why would he risk being caught by returning it?"

"It's 3:00 a.m. There was no reason to suspect anyone would hear him. But your question is a good one. Why?" He poked the wallet back into the bag. "I'll take it to the police tomorrow and have them check for prints."

"I can do it."

He heard the I-am-a-perfectly-capable-woman tone in her voice. "I'd like to tag along, if you don't mind. I don't think you should be wandering on your own just yet."

"Taking the bus to the police station isn't exactly wandering."

Not an ounce of fear shone in her eyes now.

"But I'd be glad for your company, Chase."

"Good. I'll drive."

They climbed back into their respective beds. Too wound up to sleep, Chase lay there, sorting what he knew about Bobby, trying to decide if he might have a connection with Dodger, who would have been Chase's first choice of suspect, given his record of assault against women. Something wasn't clicking with the theory that the crime was random, but—

An important piece of the puzzle fell into place. Satisfied with his conclusion, he finally let himself sleep.

"The ski mask," Chase said to Leslie later that morning. Tessa sat in a chair beside him in one of the police interrogation rooms. "That's the missing link. How could it be a crime of opportunity when he had a ski mask, Les?"

"It could still be random. He may have intended harm toward someone, but not necessarily Tessa. Nothing else makes sense, Chase. She'd completely broken her routine, which you can hardly call routine, anyway, since she's lived there only for a week." The intercom buzzed, interrupting them.

"Bobby Moran's come in, along with an attorney," Leslie said, standing. "You two move into the observation room. You can watch from there while I question him."

Tessa hated all this police business, even though Leslie was doing everything possible to make it bearable. She felt raw. Not only from the visible injuries but deep inside, in a place where no one could see. She was angry that she'd let her guard slip because she'd been so anxious to get to work, to see Chase. She was embarrassed that Chase had seen her at her worst. She'd left her parents' home because she wanted a normal life, an independent life, then within the first week, both goals had been shattered.

She'd given in to Chase's protection too easily. She'd decided that during the night. She didn't like that he'd seen her vulnerable.

"Tired?" he asked as they waited in the adjoining room. He slid a hand under her hair to rub her neck.

She nodded. It was a good enough excuse.

"When we're done here, we'll go to the Center. You can take a nap upstairs in my place."

"No. I want to work."

He moved behind her. Both hands now massaged her neck and shoulders. "You're hard on yourself. What could you have done differently yesterday?"

She'd gone over the scenario a hundred times in her head. "Been more alert. Not taken the shortcut."

They came to attention as people moved into the interrogation room—Leslie, the attorney and Bobby. They all sat at the table. Tessa studied him. He was definitely the right height and body type. No rings; right kind of watchband. His shirt advertised a popular beer.

"I have advised my client to answer your questions, Inspector," the lawyer said. "He doesn't have anything to hide."

"Good. So, Bobby, where were you yesterday morning about five-fifty?"

"Out."

"Specifically."

"Walkin' the 'hood. Checkin' things. You know."

"Did you see anything unusual?"

"Sorta."

After a few long seconds, Leslie leaned forward. "Don't tick me off, Bobby."

"I saw that woman from the Center get knocked down. She was askin' for it, you know?"

"Asking for what?"

He gave her a don't-be-stupid look. "For to be grabbed."

"Why do you say that?"

"Look, lady, any woman who looks like she does shouldn't be walkin' alone. All that long, pretty hair? And those dresses she likes to wear? She's just beggin' for trouble."

"Do you know who knocked her down?"

"Nope. Couldn't tell who was behind that mask."

Tessa stiffened. So, he really had seen what happened. Or maybe he was trying to shift blame.

"Why didn't you try to help her?"

He snorted. "That woman don't need no help from me or nobody. She took care of herself just fine."

"In fact, she handles herself so well, she ended up embarrassing you last week, didn't she? Your pride was stung. Maybe you wanted to get back at her."

"Maybe. But it wasn't me who jumped her."

"You told Mr. Ryan that the woman wouldn't be so lucky next time."

Bobby shifted in his chair. "I was just spoutin', you know? I didn't mean nothin' by it. I don't hurt women. That's my rule."

"You tried to snatch her purse last week."

"Yeah, but I wouldn'ta hurt her. Only jerks hurt women."

Leslie leaned back. A considering look came over her face. "You left her purse at her door last night."

"I picked it up. So what? Better me than somebody else. I saw it there after they both went running in different directions. I figured someone else'd come along and she'd never see it again."

"Your fingerprints are on her wallet."

He crossed his arms over his chest. "She owed me a reward. She's got a job. Won't hurt her to be out a few bucks."

Leslie stared at him until he fidgeted. "Wait here," she said to the lawyer.

She came into the observation room a minute later, Tessa's

purse in hand. "They're done checking for prints. Look through it and see if anything is missing besides the money."

"Do you believe him, Les?" Chase asked.

"I'm inclined to. His story certainly has a ring of truth. But the other two times we pulled him in, he seemed honest, too. He might just be that good at lying."

"Everything is here," Tessa said. She set the bag down. "Maybe nothing was worth taking except the cash."

"Maybe. But if that were the case, I don't think he'd return the bag, do you? And if you can't identify him, we can't hold him."

"I can't. Unless he has that odor about him. And I was really close to him when I had him against the car hood. I didn't notice it then."

"Maybe just the ski mask smelled, not the man," Chase said.

Leslie shrugged. "We don't have enough cause to hold him."

"Where are his parents? Why isn't one of them here with him?" Tessa asked.

"He lives with his father, who refuses to do anything beyond making sure a lawyer is present. It's sad, isn't it? He's got means beyond the other kids, but what kind of a chance does he have if his father won't give him his attention? He's screaming to be noticed."

"Can I talk to him?" Tessa asked. She felt Chase stiffen behind her and knew he didn't approve.

"I don't see why not. Chase, you'd better stay here or he'll think we're ganging up on him."

Belligerent. Tessa summed up Bobby's expression in a second. She'd no more than walked through the door when his face assumed the hostile look, although whether it was genuine or his personal mask she didn't know. He was only fourteen. Too young to have given up.

"I wanted to thank you for returning my bag," she said, remaining standing. "Usually, though, when someone does a good deed, they don't choose their own reward."

"Would you've given me the money?"

"Probably not. Not all of it, anyway."

His shoulders lifted in a so-there shrug.

"If I hadn't been able to get away yesterday, would you have helped me, Bobby?"

He stared at her in return for a few seconds, then, "He got you good, huh. You gonna have scars?"

Tessa touched her cheek lightly. "I don't think so. The scrapes aren't that deep." She put her fist to her heart. "Here, though. He took something from me. Something more valuable than money."

"Welcome to the real world, lady. That ain't no ivory tower out there."

"I know. Maybe more than you, I know."

He frowned.

"Anyway, I just wanted to thank you. Oh, and I understand that Mr. Ryan invited you to come to the Center. I hope you do, Bobby. He's set up some tough rules, but they're worth it. You can feel safe there."

Bobby shifted his bored glance to Leslie. "Can I go now?"

"Yeah."

"Remind you of anyone?" Chase asked Leslie when he came into the room after Bobby and the lawyer left.

"Sort of. You were defensive, too, but not hostile."

"He's not beyond hope," Chase said, staring out the door. "It's got to be now, though. Something's kept him out of a gang so far, but it can't last forever. That was a decent thing he did— bringing Tessa's bag to her. Even if he did take the money first."

A few minutes later Chase and Tessa headed for the parking lot.

"Do you think the attack was random?" Chase asked her after they climbed into his van.

"Do you?"

"I asked first."

She smiled then, which erased the worry from her face and

softened her gaze. He could've lost himself in all that softness last night. He needed to decide, and soon, how far this relationship was going to go. She was a white-picket-fence kind of woman, and he'd been surrounded by cement walls for so long that he didn't know if he could adjust to the openness and freedom she offered. He only knew she tempted him too much.

"Yes, I think it was random," she said finally. "What do you think?"

"I'm leaning that direction. I don't suppose you'd let me take you to and from the Center for a while?" He slid the key into the ignition but didn't start the engine. "Don't frown at me, Miss Rose. I knew what your answer was going to be. But I had to ask."

"Ever the gentleman."

"You say that with a hint of disgust, Tessa. Why?"

She folded her arms and looked out the windshield. "Maybe I don't want you to be a perfect gentleman around me. Maybe I wouldn't mind a little chauvinistic attitude once in a while."

"Yet you don't want me to escort you to work and home."

"I didn't say it was logical. I've given up trying to find the logic in this relationship." She looked at him then. "I'm mostly glad that we—you—didn't let things get out of hand last night."

"Mostly?"

"As you said before, everything's happening fast. It's exciting. I can't think of much else, frankly. But..."

He waited until he realized she was going to leave the word there hanging. "But that doesn't make it right."

"It feels right."

He heard the unspoken *but* this time. "You've used the words *maybe* and *mostly*, Tessa. Until you tell me *yes* and *completely*, you're safe."

"There's that word again. *Safe*," she murmured, a pondering tone to her voice. "So, you're saying that I'm the one in charge, here. I'm the one who's calling the shots, making the decisions, taking the responsibility. What if I don't want to be solely responsible?''

''I'm willing to exert influence.'' He pushed a lever, sending his seat back as far as it could go, then he grabbed her hand and pulled her into his lap, letting her back rest against the driver-side window. ''I've been wanting to do this all morning.''

''Why, Chase Ryan, there is a little bit of the caveman in you.''

He curved his hands into her hair, against her head, and dragged her to him. And then he plundered.

Tessa was pleased. And thrilled. And staggeringly happy. She didn't care that they were in a police parking lot, that they were visible through the windshield for anyone to observe. She'd wanted to kiss him all morning, too.

It was worth the wait. His mouth tasted dangerous, a rich, dark wine of pleasure. She pulled back a little, then framed his face with her hands. Oh, he looked so handsome, his eyes silvery with passion, the planes and angles of his face hardened like granite. Even his thighs were unyielding under her rear. She pressed her lips to his eyes, closing them before they saw too deeply into her soul. It was getting harder and harder to resist him—and easier and easier to ignore what could tear them apart. If she could get away with never telling him—

His hands banded her arms, pushing her back. The steering wheel pressed against her. She watched his gaze drift down her. The look alone made the tips of her breasts tighten even more painfully.

''You're like something out of my dreams. My life has been empty of softness. Women—'' he hesitated ''—I've had a purpose in life. It has never included this.''

''This?''

''*This*. You. You're different from any other woman I've known. But my path was set a long time ago.''

''You haven't allowed for any detours?''

''I don't have much to offer.''

''You have plenty to offer. But I don't have expectations

Chase. I'm enjoying this as much as you are. Let's not complicate it with problems that don't exist.'' She moved back to the passenger seat.

He started the engine. ''I'd still feel better if you let me take you to and from the Center.''

''I know.''

''But the answer's still no.''

''On that particular question.''

He shifted into reverse, but before he backed the van out, he gave her a long, searching look. She smiled.

''You're enjoying yourself, aren't you, Tessa?''

''Oh, yes. I am definitely enjoying myself. And so are you.'' Even without seeing him smile in return, she knew that for a fact.

# Seven

Sarge was waiting for them in Chase's office. Tessa felt her cheeks heat as he studied her injured face, then he inspected Chase just as thoroughly. She finally tossed a grin Chase's way.

"I think we have to salute," she whispered dramatically. "Or we're going to pull latrine duty."

A half smile lifted one corner of Sarge's mouth. "If you're cocky enough to make jokes at my expense, Miss Rose, then I guess I can stop worrying."

"I'm fine, thanks." She took Chase's hand and squeezed. "I'm going to get to work. Thank you for taking me this morning. I like your friend, Leslie. She made the situation a whole lot easier."

"Les is good at her job."

"She thinks the world of you, too. I have to admire her taste." Smiling, Tessa said goodbye.

Chase closed the door. He needed a few minutes alone. He needed to sort some things out. Instead, he had to face Sarge.

"Well?" the older man asked.

"She got hurt. She handled it."

"Grace under fire."

Chase nodded. "So, how'd you hear?" He dropped into his chair, suddenly bone tired. He glanced at the stack of message slips, then ignored them.

"Once a cop, always a cop."

"Someone notified you?"

"Leslie O'Keefe." Sarge settled into the chair across the desk. "I always liked that girl."

Chase leaned back. He heard the implied message in Sarge's words, because he'd heard it before. "That girl, as you call her, is still in love with her ex-husband. Even if that weren't the case, there wouldn't be anything between us but history and friendship, the same as with Gabe and Ben and Sebastian. And you. She's one of the guys to me."

"Yeah, well, we all know what a fool Ben was to let her go. It's just that I want you to have more in your life than this place. You've done what you set out to do, son. You've made it a success. Now it's time to look at doing the same for yourself."

"I seem to be, whether I want to or not."

"Tessa Rose."

"Tessa Rose," Chase repeated. Soft, smiling, fragrant, *strong* Tessa Rose.

"You hardly know her."

"It's a relationship that's running under its own power, Sarge. I can't stop it. It's just rolling down the tracks like some runaway train without any brakes."

"Are you hearing the danger you're describing? The crash could be crippling."

"But not fatal. Why does this bother you so much? You've been pushing me for years to have more of a social life. The minute I get one, you change your mind?"

The older man leaned forward, concern lining a new map on

his craggy face. "You've never been head over heels before. That can be dangerous."

"It feels *good*." Weariness blanketed Chase, along with concern for Tessa's safety and an overwhelming need to make love to her, to keep her beside him.

Nobody knew more about the risk he was taking than he did. Not Ben. Not Gabe. Not Leslie. Not even Sarge. Chase had stopped taking risks a long time ago, deciding it was better to be alone than to be hurt—at least where women were concerned. But a new, deep yearning had coiled around him the moment he'd set eyes on the beautiful preschool teacher he thought could probably teach him a thing or two herself.

He wanted to travel that new road.

"I've said my piece," Sarge said, slapping his hands on his thighs. "Now, tell me what happened yesterday."

Someone was watching her. Tessa looked over her shoulder as she walked the final block to her apartment, but she didn't see anyone paying particular attention to her. She clutched her shopping bags closer, impatience to get home battling anxiety at the prickling sensations that set her heart pumping, loud and fast.

She'd made it safely to and from the Center during the work week, although she'd varied her routine a little with each trip—and she'd had company most of the time. Today was Saturday, however. No routine. No work. Just the lovely anticipation of a Saturday night date for dinner and a movie with Chase. She'd spent the morning preparing a dense, fudgy chocolate cake for a late-night dessert, wanting an excuse to invite him in, knowing how he loved chocolate.

Tessa darted a look behind her again as she started up her apartment steps, then hurried into the building, up the stairs and on into the welcoming security of her own apartment. She dropped her bag on the couch and rushed to the window. Nothing out of the ordinary caught her eye. After a few minutes, she gave up her intensive search. Must've been her imagination.

Six hours to kill before Chase would pick her up. She could iron her new dress, decide on the accessories, indulge in a leisurely bubble bath early because her hair took so long to air-dry.

She dumped the contents of her shopping expedition onto the couch. Silky undergarments in a rainbow of colors lay like an exotic dancer's discarded scarves tossed with wild abandon. She snipped price tags, then folded each item carefully before putting them in the dresser, leaving out only a pair of white lacy panties and a strapless, backless bustier appliquéd with matching lace. The off-the-shoulder, white eyelet dress she'd chosen was cut low enough to offer a tantalizing view of cleavage, the scalloped hem would brush her calves with each step. As unsophisticated as it looked, it was the most daring thing she'd ever owned—not counting the new underwear.

Too wound up to relax in the tub for long, she finally drained it and took a shower, conditioning and combing her hair before she got out. When dry, it would blanket her back with springy curls she hoped would be irresistible to him.

Unable to wait a minute longer to see how she would look, she dressed as if it was time, instead of four hours early. Her damp hair brushing against her skin sent shivers through her, but she stopped noticing as soon as she looked in the mirror.

Oh, yes. This was the right choice.

She smiled, deciding she wouldn't wear any jewelry except some simple gold hoop earrings and one gold bangle bracelet, a sixteenth-birthday gift. As she unfastened the row of buttons down the front of her dress, she moved to the window and peered out the blinds again, wondering how to pass the time. She wouldn't be able to sleep. She didn't want to clean house now that she had bathed.

Not for the first time, she wished for the book she'd been too embarrassed to buy in Chase's presence. What *did* men need? And how would she know for sure? She didn't want to make any mistakes. Of course, he would undoubtedly take the lead when it finally happened. It. Making love. Would it be good between them? Awkward? Difficult? She had too many questions that she couldn't answ—

Tessa stopped unbuttoning her dress as she focused on a man lurking near a house across the street. A man with buzz-cut gray hair and military posture. Sarge.

So, Chase was having her watched. Guarded. Even when she'd specifically told him she'd handle it on her own. She'd thought the group of teenagers who'd walked home with her each night had initiated the protective gesture themselves. They'd certainly been angry about the attack against her and solicitous about her welfare. But it was obviously Chase who'd rounded up his own security force, figuring she wouldn't ever know.

A tiny—infinitesimal—part of her was grateful. On the other hand, he'd gone completely against her wishes. She'd lived in fear almost all her life. Her parents had seen to that. She couldn't live like that anymore—it was why she'd left home. She knew there were dangers, but she refused to let them dominate her life or imprison her in her home—or anywhere else, for that matter.

The longer she thought about it, the angrier she got. Really! He had some nerve! He could have just insisted, and maybe she would have given in. Wasn't it just like a man? He'd *man*euvered and *man*ipulated and *man*aged and...and...whatever other *man*-words applied.

Well, she wasn't waiting until six o'clock to deal with it. She wasn't going to spend almost four hours getting angrier and more agitated by the minute. She'd have it out with him right now.

Not even stopping to change, she scooped up her purse and left her apartment. She strode out the front door, down the steps and across the street. Sarge swallowed visibly, but his posture never faltered.

"Miss Rose."

"Mr. Buckley. You might as well walk with me instead of skulking around behind me, making we wonder if I'm being followed or losing my mind."

"Ah—"

"Don't give me that innocent look. I know you followed me today. I'm going to the Center. I'm inviting you along." She walked away. In a few seconds, he came up beside her.

"You look nice," he said.

"Thank you." Her daring, off-the-shoulder white dress made her feel as out of place as a nun in a strip joint.

"Got a date?"

"As if you didn't know."

"Why would I know?"

"Chase didn't tell you we were going out?"

"Chase keeps his own counsel. Even more so since you came into his life."

She eyed the man, who looked straight ahead. "You resent that."

He hesitated. "No. I've wanted him to find someone special."

"Just not me."

"You already know my reservations, Miss Rose."

It occurred to her she hadn't put on any makeup or dabbed her pulse points with perfume. And her hair was still damp, so it clung to her skin where it touched, sticking there. And the pretty sandals she'd intended to wear were nestled in the shoe box resting on her coffee table. On her feet, instead, were her sneakers with the painted teddy bears and balloons. Suddenly she regretted her impetuous decision. She would see him in a few hours, after all. They could have their fight then as well as now.

She slowed her Olympic pace enough that Sarge finally looked at her. "Something wrong?"

The worst of it was, she hadn't paid any attention whatsoever to her surroundings. She'd relinquished that responsibility to Sarge without giving it a second thought. Instead, she'd let emotion shove her common sense aside. Again.

Well, that was just another thing to be mad at Chase about!

"Everything's wrong," she almost growled, then picked up speed again until they reached the Center. The minute they entered the building, she dismissed Sarge. She kept going, one long stride after another, until she reached Chase's office.

She slammed the door behind her and marched to his desk.

Chase watched her approach, angelic and avenging at the same time. She planted her hands on his desk and leaned toward him. His gaze shifted down. His mouth went dry. "I'll have to call you back, Gabe," he said into the phone, then hung up. Buying himself time, he made a show of looking at his watch. "I wasn't supposed to pick you up until six."

"Is that all you have to say?"

"What do you want me to say, Tessa?" He was fascinated by the fierce expression on her face, by the fiery sparks in her eyes, by the deepening color in her cheeks. By her breasts that teased and tantalized him as they were pushed to soft, tempting mounds of flesh above her low neckline. It was all he could do to return his gaze to her face.

"I want you to acknowledge me as a competent adult."

He frowned. "I do. What makes you think otherwise?"

"I told you I was capable of getting myself to work and home."

"I remember. So?"

"So, the army of special agents you enlisted has got to go. I thought I was being followed! It was only Sarge. I don't want a bodyguard, Chase."

He stood finally and moved around the desk. She straightened, folding her arms under her breasts as she awaited him.

"I didn't assign anyone to guard you," he said, dazzled by her anger, shocked that his body was reacting so powerfully to this whole new side of her.

"I'm supposed to believe that?" she said, sputtering. "My independence is important to me. I don't want you to interfere in what I'm accomplishing."

Chase needed to kiss her, needed to channel all that passion in another direction—toward him, still, but not in anger. For days he'd ignored his fantasies, ignored them all by finding a well of control he must have been saving for this very occasion.

"Come with me," he said.

She opened her mouth.

"Not a word, Tessa. Not a single word."

He took her hand, not letting go as they navigated the halls to the back of the building, then finally ended up in his apartment, the door locked, the world shut out.

He faced her squarely. "First. No one questions my integrity. If I say I had nothing to do with whoever has been following you or guarding you, *I had nothing to do with it.* I don't know what you're talking about, except that I can guess. The kids probably decided you needed protection. Sarge undoubtedly came to the same conclusion. No one discussed it with me."

He took a step closer. "Second. I want you."

Pinned by his gaze, Tessa went perfectly still. The heat of anger went up in a puff of smoke, replaced in a heartbeat with fire, hot and dangerous and exciting. "I want you, too."

He drew her hand to the placket of his jeans, then molded her fingers over him. He sucked in a reactionary breath as she slid her hand along him, up and down, up and down, up and— "Anger's not supposed to do this," he said.

"Touch me," she whispered, "and see where the anger took *me.*"

He held her gaze. With both hands, he bunched up her skirt to her waist and pulled her close. She blinked slowly as he slid a hand down, under the band of her panties, into the hot, damp nest.

"Chase," she breathed.

"You are incredible." He slid his fingers lower, could feel her pulse pound there. "When you stormed into my office, I thought I'd never seen anything so beautiful in all my life. I know it's a cliché. I know it sounds like a line. But it's the truth."

She moaned as he found the core of her femininity with the pad of his finger.

"Not yet," he said, low and hungry. "Not yet. Let's go to the bedroom."

She followed him, her hand tightly holding his, her mind barely registering her surroundings. She noticed books, lots and lots of books, and a big bed and open blinds that slanted stripes of sunlight across his quilt, which he flung aside, leaving only a huge, inviting expanse of sheet and two pillows.

And then he kissed her, and she could tell he was trying not to plunder or dominate or deny her the chance to respond. "Don't hold back," she whispered. "I don't want you to hold back."

He attacked her mouth. She attacked back. His hands tangled in her hair, lifting it, crushing it, pushing it back, tipping her head to expose her neck. He nibbled the flesh there, stroked it with his tongue. She felt him begin to unbutton her dress and she knew she had to stop him for a minute, to tell him.

*I'm in love with you.* The words wouldn't come—couldn't come—not until there was only truth between them. But there was something else she could say. She waited until he finished unbuttoning her and let her dress fall to the floor, leaving her wearing the not-so-innocent-looking undergarments and the silly shoes. He bent to pick up her dress and lay it aside. She toed off the shoes.

"Perfect," he said, reverence in his voice as he ran his fingers across the flesh revealed above her bustier.

"Chase."

He met her gaze as his fingers dipped into her cleavage.

"I kind of haven't ever done this before," she said.

The most amazing thing happened then. He smiled. Chase Ryan smiled. And it changed his whole face. His eyes lightened to silver, his jaw softened, his lips looked even more kissable. Unable to resist, she pulled his head down and pressed her lips to his.

"I haven't either," he said, just as their kiss began to deepen.

"You haven't?"

He shook his head, his smile still in place. "I figure we know enough about the mechanics to muddle through it all right, though.''

She knew. She knew why he was a virgin. She wouldn't have to ask him. Yet he'd be curious if she didn't. Now what?

''Since this is a first for both of us, how about we try to take our time,'' he said, unhooking the first of eight hooks down her bustier. Then the next. And the next. ''Did you wear this for me?''

She nodded.

''It's not even my birthday,'' he said.

''It's mine.''

''No. Your birthday was last month.''

He peeled off the lacy garment, laying it aside, then he pushed the delicate panties down and off her.

She sighed as she stood nude before him, feeling only a little shy. Too much admiration shimmered in his eyes to allow her to be overly hesitant. ''I'm declaring it my new birthday. Because I feel like I've just been born.''

''That's a beautiful birthday suit you're wearing.''

She smiled. ''I'm kind of anxious to see yours.''

''Then you should get busy unwrapping.''

''I'm one of those people who takes her time. I ease the ribbon off the package first.'' She pulled his shirt over his head. ''I peel off the tape, one piece at a time.'' She unfastened each button of his jeans with exaggerated care. He kicked off his shoes before she tugged the denim down his long legs. ''Then I spread open the paper and look at the box. I want to know what's inside but the anticipation feels good, too, so I wait a minute and just look.'' He wore only gray cotton briefs now, and his own anticipation was evident.

''Finally I lift the lid to see what's waiting for me.'' He was as naked as she now, but so boldly different. Hard and muscular beyond her expectation. Solid and sturdy and all man. All vigorous, virile man. ''Happy birthday to me,'' she singsonged, trying to smile but barely able to speak.

*Destiny.* Again the word found its place in her heart and mind. This was what she'd been waiting for. This inevitability. This rightness. This magic. He was everything. Her past. Her present. Her future. Her universe. There would never be anyone else.

Breathing his name, she laid her cheek against his shoulder, wrapped her arms around him and burrowed there, feeling the safety and warmth of his returning embrace. She didn't know how long they stood, body to body, soul speaking silently to soul, but long enough to stop the world on its axis.

Chase pulled her a little closer, not understanding how he could feel so much, so deeply, so fast, but as committed to this woman as any man could ever be to any woman. "We should discuss birth control," he said finally, knowing it was the last mundane item they needed to deal with.

"I'm not on the Pill. But I don't believe there's any risk."

"I can use protection."

"I don't think it's necessary. But if it makes you feel better, safer..."

He realized that the consequences wouldn't bother him. He'd waited all these years for the right woman, never believing that she existed, never believing he was worthy of sharing a physical relationship, much less an entire life. All it had taken was the right woman to change his mind.

"I'm willing to chance it," he said.

After a long, searching kiss, he guided her to lie on the bed. "I have imagined you here like this," he said, stretching out beside her, spreading her hair across the pillow. "From the first day that I met you, I've wanted you in my bed. And here you are, looking like more than my dreams. You have the most perfect body." He cupped her breast and took a pebbled nipple into his mouth as she arched and moaned. Reaction sizzled through him, low and fiery. He didn't know how long he could wait, how long he could stretch out the experience to make a memory, especially when she was writhing and groaning and saying his name like that—all hoarse and inviting.

"Maybe we should go slow the *second* time," she said haltingly as he nudged his knee between hers and moved her legs apart. She jumped when he touched her intimately, not sliding a hand down her, not teasing her with his mouth, just resting his fingers against her where she throbbed and burned for him.

She wrapped a hand around his erection. "So hot," she whispered. "So strong. I love touching you. I can't wait to feel you filling me up."

"Tessa." He barely got her name out as she did wonderful things with her fingers. He pushed her hand away, then moved over her, demanding a kiss that obliterated every previous kiss. He dragged his mouth down the side of her neck, caught a nipple with his teeth and scraped the hard tip before he sucked it deep into his mouth. She called his name again, spreading her legs wider, inviting him in. Rising up on his hands, he pressed himself to the entrance.

She opened her eyes. "Yes."

Such a simple word. The answer to all the questions he wanted to ask.

He pushed forward. She squinted. He slipped into her slick warmth, felt her muscles contract around him, waited until she relaxed. Sweat beaded his forehead.

"Just do it," she said.

Which made him slow down even more, made him more determined that they remember this singular moment. He smiled. Tears sprang to her eyes when he did. It seemed like the most serious moment in his life, and yet it was the most joyous.

He pressed farther, finding resistance, knowing that it wasn't a barrier for her alone, but for him, too. He didn't know why it was called a loss of innocence. He'd lost his innocence a long time ago. It was a celebration of life, however.

He wasn't aware of seconds or minutes. He only knew when he was one with her. Happiness wrapped around him. Happiness and exultation and bliss. He felt her tighten, squeezing him rhyth-mically, heard her surprised gasp followed by a flattering moan and her fingers digging into him. Then he finally, finally, let himself follow. And it was beautiful beyond words.

# Eight

**H**e offered her one of his shirts to wear—provided she didn't button it—as evening brought a cool ocean breeze through the city. Tessa wondered what good that would do since she was pretty much exposed unless she buttoned it.

"It's a compromise," he said.

"Not much of one."

"Okay, then. You can fasten one button."

She laughed—and decided not to bother. One wouldn't do much good, after all. She raked him with her gaze. He leaned against the kitchen counter watching her pour two glasses of iced tea. He was wearing his cutoffs, because she asked him to, but she could see that he was impressively aroused, anyway. She started to pass his glass to him, then set it low against him instead.

"Won't work," he said, swiping the glass from her. "Nothing's going to make me want you less."

"Flattery will get you everywhere."

"Back in bed?"

She sipped her tea as she eyed his hopeful look. They'd moved from the bed to the bathtub, after which they'd had to mop the water off the floor. So much for going slowly the second time.

"You're blushing," he said, setting his drink aside, moving in on her. He pressed her against the counter before lifting her to sit there.

Ladylike, she kept her knees together and her ankles crossed as she tugged the shirt closed. She traced her fingers across his lips. "I wasn't sure you knew how to smile."

"Out of the habit, I guess." Urging her legs apart, he moved between them, opened her shirt and tucked the fabric behind her back. "Better put that glass down before you drop it."

She took his advice, then finger-combed his hair, enjoying his open admiration. He wasn't touching her yet, which somehow made it more intimate. Her nipples responded in a way that obviously pleased him, as he finally ran his palms over them.

"So, is sex everything you hoped it would be?" she asked, her voice hitching a little. *Was it worth all the years you denied yourself the pleasure?* she wondered silently.

"*You* were."

"You are an expert at the politically correct answer, Mr. Ryan."

Busy indulging his own fantasies, he didn't respond right away, then asked, "Are you asking why it was my first time?"

"No."

The word came out harsh enough that he met her gaze.

"I don't want to know. Not now. Not yet. This is a magical time, and I have the feeling that the reality of our pasts—the reasons why neither of us had been intimate before—will break the spell. Can't we just enjoy each other for the weekend?"

"You'll get no argument from me. Except that I do have to explain, Tessa. My past is a big part of who I am. It's important that you know." Chase picked up his glass of iced tea, cold and wet with condensation. He pressed it between her legs and listened to her suck in a hard, fast breath.

"Feel good?" he asked.

She gave a little moan as he pulled her toward him more, toward the edge of the counter, leaving her vulnerable in a way she hadn't been before. "It's...it's good. Soothing. And yet more than that."

"Are you that tender?" He tipped the glass, turning it at the same time, sending the cooling relief to a different part of her. He looked at her face then. There was so much yet to discover. He was aware of her natural shyness over the newness, but he didn't want to waste a minute, especially on unnecessary hesitance. "You're blushing again."

"Am I?" she asked, breathless.

He plunked the glass on the counter, then fished out an ice cube. "Close your eyes."

He traced a map of icy streams over the gentle slopes of her breasts, onto the rigid peaks, down her softly rounded abdomen, and finally into the tempting delta below, where it melted completely. She wriggled, making wonderful sounds in her throat that built, second by second, touch by touch.

"Chase. Let's go back to bed."

The urgency in her voice flattered him.

The last light of day filtered through his bedroom window and onto the bed. He unzipped his shorts and kicked them off as he watched her shrug his shirt off her shoulders and kneel on the sheets.

"I don't want to hurt you," he said before joining her on the bed. "You're sore already. We'll just take it slow, okay? Maybe that'll help."

"Okay."

Uncertainty rang in the single word, as if she couldn't believe he wasn't in a hurry. He reined in his need, knowing she should be fully aroused in order to lessen the pain. He may not have any practical experience, but he'd read about how to make love to a woman, studied it in unendingly curious detail, hoping the day would come, never really believing it would. He'd stored away so many fantasies, so many wishes, all denied for so very long.

He invited her to take control, to straddle him and take him within her when she felt ready. It gave him a whole new view of her as her breasts swayed within reach of his mouth, a temptation he couldn't resist—didn't have to resist. She was every fantasy come to life as she moved against him, electricity crackling between their bodies as she slid herself along his length, becoming more bold with every glide.

Tessa opened her eyes and looked at him, shocked at the climax that threatened at their contact. She hadn't known...

She stopped moving abruptly, held her breath for a minute, and then she mated with him. For the moment. And for life.

He was right. The tenderness all but disappeared, replaced with building sensation as she found a rhythm of pleasure. She leaned over him, letting him suckle her, listening to his sandpapery words of encouragement.

She felt such a connection with him, beyond physical, beyond mental, even beyond emotional. It all melded to create a dimension she never would have believed existed, a plane she reached only because her mind and heart and soul converged with the shattering climax she shared with him.

*I love you, Chase. I love you. Do you love me? Are you feeling this, too?* The words swirled and brightened, obliterating long-held visions of another time and place where this beautiful act hadn't been beautiful at all.

She clung to him—because the loveliness that replaced the harrowing image overwhelmed her. And because he hadn't allowed her to free her imprisoned words by offering his own. And because she was beginning to realize how difficult loving him was going to be. His past was linked with hers, for better or for worse. And now so was his present. Their futures depended on how well she handled what faced them.

Too exhausted to think about it anymore, she stretched out beside him, the burden of her secret weighing heavily on her.

"Something wrong?" he asked.

"No. Nothing."

Chase pulled her into his arms. She confused him. Her mood swung high and low and everywhere in between. For all her softness, for all the light that shone from her eyes, she carried something dark inside her that she masked well. Fragments of the darkness floated up at odd times—during tender moments and passionate ones, times when he would have expected her to become even softer.

"The reality of our pasts...will break the spell." Her words came back to him suddenly. Meaning what? Wasn't she as curious about why he'd never made love before as he was about her? It was a rarity these days, but especially for a thirty-two-year-old man.

Nothing about this relationship was simple, he realized. The only certainty was the penance he'd been paying for eighteen years. He was ready to give it up, to take a step forward, to live a normal life. The question was, would he be allowed to?

Tessa figured she had about fifteen minutes before Chase returned from the bakery, where he'd gone to pick up their Sunday-morning breakfast. They'd showered together, but given her lack of available wardrobe, she debated between putting her dress on or continuing to wear his shirt.

She decided to get dressed—so that he could undress her. She'd just slipped into her panties and bustier when she heard his key in the lock. Well, shoot.

"You're too early," she called out. Flinging his shirt on, she headed out the bedroom door and crashed right into a man. A tall, dark and handsome stranger who smiled slowly as he watched her clutch the shirt to her.

"Good morning," he said, taking in all of her in one sweeping gaze.

"Who are you?"

"Gabriel Marquez. Who are you?"

"Oh. You're Gabe." She straightened her shoulders as he made a point of putting his house key away. She didn't extend her hand. "I'm Tessa Rose."

He seemed to be examining the scrapes on her face.

"A pleasure to meet you, Miss Rose. Where's Chase? He wasn't downstairs."

"He went to the bakery. Would you like some coffee?"

"That would be great, thanks."

"You probably know where the mugs are," she said. "I'll just put something on...."

He grinned and turned away. Tessa hurried into her dress, debated about her teacher sneakers, then decided to go barefoot. She looked in the mirror. Her hair had seen tamer moments. She didn't have on any makeup, of course, but her cheeks were pink and her lips a well-kissed rose color. Gabe had obviously drawn his own conclusions, so there was no use hiding out until Chase returned and sent him on his way.

Feeling much like a gypsy with her bare feet, daring dress and wild hair, she left the bedroom. She found Gabe in the living room, sipping from a mug, holding a framed photograph. He turned it toward her.

"We were fifteen when this was taken," he said. "The unlikeliest five friends imaginable."

She came up beside him and looked at the photograph. "I've met Ben and Leslie. You have the same smile now as then. Chase looks just as serious. Who's the other boy?"

"Sebastian Blackstone."

"His name makes him sound dangerous."

"Does it? Nothing could be further from the truth. He's the most easygoing, and the one who keeps us together. So, you teach here, right?"

"Yes." She was bothered by the way Gabe looked at her, deeply, too deeply, as if tapping into her soul with his intense, dark eyes. His face was classically handsome, but there was more there. Complexity, a whole lot of living, some pain, as well.

Whatever he was about to say got lost when a key was jammed into the lock and the door opened.

"I hope you're naked," Chase called out, "because I plan to drip the jelly from my doughnut on you and lick—"

The rest of the sentence jammed in his throat when he saw Tessa—and Gabe—staring at him, Tessa with her mouth gaping, Gabe grinning wickedly.

"He had a key," Tessa said weakly, her cheeks flaming. "Excuse me," she whispered before hurrying out of the room. She slammed the bedroom door shut behind her.

"Well, I don't want to keep you from your...breakfast," Gabe said.

Chase smiled unwillingly, hoping he didn't look like he was strutting, particularly in front of the champion playboy of the western world.

Gabe swore, an amazed tone coating his words. "So that's how it is. She's already changed you."

"I don't want to talk about it with you."

"Why not?"

He shrugged. "It's personal."

With a nod Gabe acknowledged Chase's right to privacy.

"I won't be playing basketball tonight," Chase said. "Will you let Ben know?"

"Sure. See you next week."

"Gabe? What did you want, anyway?"

"You didn't return my call yesterday. I heard from Sebastian's doctor. He doesn't think the paralysis is permanent."

Chase closed his eyes for a few seconds. "Thank God."

"And the miracles of modern medicine. He's got a long road ahead of him, though."

"I'd like to see him."

"It's safer this way, Chase. You know that. He can't afford the risk of any of us being followed there. I'll let you know if anything changes."

Gabe left then, leaving Chase to consider what kind of mood

he'd find Tessa in now. Embarrassed, certainly, judging by her expression when she dashed away.

He knocked lightly on the bedroom door, waiting until she called for him to come in before he turned the knob. He found her sitting cross-legged on the bed, her white skirt a cloud around her.

He tried to gauge her expression. "Gabe must have parked out front. I came through the alley." He sat beside her, facing her. "He doesn't drop in often. It must have been a shock for you."

"Considering I was wearing only my underwear and your shirt—unbuttoned—I'd say it was a bit of a surprise, yes."

"Gabe's the last one you need to feel embarrassment because of. They don't call him Romeo for nothing."

"Romeo? Really?"

"A nickname that stems from adolescence, mind you, but I'd say it's still valid in a lot of ways."

She grinned finally. "The look on your face when you spotted him!" Laughter bubbled up. "Jelly doughnuts, Chase?"

"So, I had a creative idea while I was walking to the bakery." He smiled as he pushed her hair over her shoulders, being gentleman enough not to comment on *her* expression before she'd run out. "Hungry?"

"Feed my stomach first, please. I'm starving."

He'd bought bagels and cream cheese, and some already-cut-up melon—and a jelly doughnut that he set on a napkin where they could both watch and anticipate. They spread their picnic on the bed as they ate and talked.

"Tell me about Gabriel Marquez," she said, before taking a long lick of cream cheese.

He watched the dollop of cream cheese disappear from her tongue into her mouth. "What do you want to know? I've already told you that we met on the first day of high school, along with Ben, Leslie and Sebastian."

"Instant friends and friends for life?"

''Not instant, exactly, but it's been steady, although we go our own ways a lot. It's complicated.''

''Meaning, you don't want to get into it.''

''Much has changed recently. Ben and Leslie got a divorce, first of all, and that's been hard on everyone. Sometimes it's uncomfortable because someone has to be excluded in an invitation to do something together. You know what, Tessa? Right at this moment, I'm more interested in stuffing that bagel down you so I can take care of a different hunger.''

She smiled with pure feminine triumph. He loved the look—but he wasn't about to give her that ammunition.

''Tell me more...about Gabe.''

He stabbed a piece of melon and fed it to her. ''What did you think of him?''

''We didn't get a chance to talk much. He has a pretty face, though.''

''Is that a compliment I should pass on?''

She leaned over and kissed him. He tasted the sweetness of cantaloupe on her lips.

''I like your face much better,'' she said. ''It has character.''

''Thank you. I think.''

She smiled. ''It was a compliment. So, what does Gabe do for a living?''

''He doesn't have a job, exactly. He's what's known as a venture capitalist.''

''He takes risks with money.''

'''Risk' is his middle name. He's got the Midas touch, though. Can't seem to lose on anything. It's funny, too, because he doesn't care about *having* money as much as he likes to just *make* it.''

''That's a world I don't understand at all. Money's always been in short supply for me.''

''Me, too. But Gabe's generous with his. He funds a lot of the stuff that goes on here. Every two years, he donates a new van. He knows I wouldn't spend money on a car for myself, but I can hardly turn down a van for the Center. It's only money, as far as he's concerned. One of these days he's going to come up against something his money won't buy. Then we'll see what he's made of.''

''A woman, I'll bet,'' she said, nodding, sure of herself. ''It'll have to be a woman. I hope I'm around to watch him deal with it.''

''I hope so, too.''

Hearing a new, serious tone in his voice, Tessa looked at him. She swallowed the last bite of her breakfast, which seemed to take forever to slide down her throat. Gone was any hint of playfulness. In its place was desire, powerful and electrifying, charging the air around them with tiny bolts of lightning.

''Would you undress for me?'' he asked tightly, urgently.

''Um.'' She blew out a breath. ''I don't know if I'm ready for that.''

''Give it a try? If you're too uncomfortable, just stop.''

''Should I have music or something?''

''If you want.'' He leaned across to the nightstand and clicked on the radio.

''I was kidding!''

Ignoring her, he fiddled with the dial until he found something appropriate, with a country-western beat.

She didn't think she could do it. But he kept talking to her, complimenting her, telling her how he felt when he looked at her, touched her, made love to her. As the song changed to a slower tune, she found some well of daring that let her throw off more of her inhibitions. She danced, she teased, she tormented. She even shimmied.

Chase stood, joining her, taking her in his arms when she wore only her silk panties and the bustier, unfastened down to the last hook. He'd never danced in his life, but she didn't seem to notice, or mind, his clumsiness. She just unbuttoned his shirt and peeled it off, then went to work on his jeans.

The music changed again, to a slow, sultry tune that matched the rising temperature in the room and the passion-building mood. Nude, finally, they continued the dance while their mouths savored and their hands caressed and their bodies moved silkily against each other. Steam rose. The air sizzled.

"I haven't even known you for two weeks," he said, looking into her eyes. His amazement at that fact increased the longer he thought about it. "Two weeks. I didn't expect something like this to happen in my lifetime, much less with someone I've known for so short a time."

"'Something like this?'"

He cupped her rear, pulling her hips snugly against his as they moved side to side in what could be called a dance only by someone with a powerful imagination. "Not only a physical relationship, but the perfection of it."

"Has it been perfect? I think you'd like me to be more daring."

"I know you've felt awkward at times." He groaned as she shifted back and forth, creating friction between them, threatening his control.

"I'm relaxing more and more. You can't expect me to lose every inhibition at once. This is exciting. But it's new, and it's a risk, no matter how good it feels."

"Does it feel good, Tessa?"

"It's indescribable. And not just this, but everything. Just being with you."

"I don't want to take you home."

"We have hours yet. Hours."

He kissed her, dragging her to her tiptoes to bring her closer still. "I feel like we should go somewhere. Do something. I don't want you to think I only want you here, naked, in my bedroom."

She smiled. "Then you'll have to stop leering at me when you say that."

He smiled back. "Well, it's my preference, but I don't want to seem like I have a one-track mind."

"I think we can forgive each other for not wanting to go out into the world this weekend."

The song ended and a commercial came on, disrupting the mood. Chase turned off the radio, then he moved Tessa until the backs of her knees touched the bed. He followed her down onto the mattress. She raised her knees, her feet flat, and he settled against her intimately.

"What's your preference for the next dance, Miss Rose?" He kissed her temple. "A waltz?" He nibbled her earlobe. "Tango?" He dragged his mouth down her neck and bit her shoulder playfully. "The twist?"

Tessa felt her skin rise in tiny bumps. He'd spent forty-five minutes arousing her. She already teetered on the brink of satisfaction, before he'd even entered her. "The polka?" she queried with exaggerated innocence.

He smiled, then he accommodated her a second later, his thrust straight and sure and bold, stretching her, filling her. She squeezed her muscles around him. He lifted his head and met her gaze when he found he couldn't withdraw. She relaxed. He pulled back, almost out, then thrust again. She tightened, imprisoning him, claiming him. He held himself still, the muscles in his face hardening, his eyes glazing. He whispered her name. She freed him, allowing him to tease her in return with a long, delicious plunge even deeper into her, making her moan and rise up. Again she made her muscles constrict, then, even though he fought it, she could feel him explode inside her, a primal burst of heat that triggered her own. Their voices echoed hoarsely, their bodies glided slickly, their mouths devoured without restraint.

Panting, Chase started to relax against her, then he felt her squeeze him again, deeply, tightly...arousingly. Shocked, he didn't move, just felt and reacted, amazed as he was consumed again by need.

"Yes," she whispered, opening and closing around him.

"But—"

"Let it take you, Chase. Let it take you."

And when he finally draped himself over her, stunned and

grateful, he felt her wriggle contentedly beneath him. He could feel her lazy smile form against his shoulder.

"Feeling pretty cocky, are you?" he asked.

"Mmm-hmm."

"I didn't know that was possible. Multiple—"

"Oh, yes. They're not just for women anymore," she murmured expertly.

He laughed. A deep, rich, joyful sound that pierced her clear through.

She'd never heard anything more wonderful in all her life.

# Nine

**G**uarding their intimacy, Chase drove her home at sunset instead of walking the five blocks, not wanting anyone else to see her. He dreaded the end of the weekend for more than one reason—she wouldn't sleep beside him tonight, all soft and warm and fragrant, and he had to explain his past to her, now.

She was quiet, too. Perhaps she was anticipating what he had to say. She'd definitely been as reluctant to leave as he was.

As soon as they were in her apartment, she disappeared into her walk-in closet to change clothes. Someone knocked on her front door.

"Would you get that, please?" she called out.

It was her across-the-hall neighbor, Norm, and a pretty young woman whom Chase hadn't met.

"Hi. Is Tess home?" Norm asked.

"She can't come to the door at the moment."

"Would you tell her that her parents dropped by about two this afternoon? They'd like her to call. I didn't tell them she was probably with you, because— Well, I figured if she wanted them to know...well, you know.''

"I'll tell her.''

"They were really upset,'' the young woman offered. "They said they'd been calling all night and all day.''

"Thank you. I'll see she gets the message.''

"I mean they were really, really upset,'' she continued.

"Come on, babe.'' Norm tugged on her arm. "We've done our job.''

Chase shut the door, then Tessa came out from the closet wearing jeans and a T-shirt.

"I heard everything,'' she said. "I suppose I'd better call before they notify the police, if they haven't already.'' She picked up the phone. "Ten messages on my answering machine. I imagine they're all from my parents. Oh, if you'd like some chocolate cake, it's under that dome. Cut me a piece, too, please.''

He found plates and forks as he listened to her try to soothe the parent on the other end. He wondered what it was like to have someone worry like that. Except for Sarge, who wasn't much of a worrier, he'd never had anyone care enough to be frantic if he decided not to come home for one night.

"I'm not going to report my whereabouts every day. We discussed this before I left home, Mom.... Well, I hadn't really planned to be gone overnight. It just worked out that way.... No, I didn't think to pick up my messages. I was busy.... I know you love me. I love you, too. But don't worry about me, okay?''

"As it turns out, they had reason to worry,'' Chase said when he hung up. He set their dessert plates on the coffee table, then returned for the two glasses of milk he'd poured. "Maybe not last night, because they couldn't know you were safe somewhere, but certainly when you were mugged.''

"I know. I can't give in to it, though, Chase. You don't know how they've sheltered me. I can't let them continue.''

He jammed his hands in his pockets. "And you don't know

how much I would have given for that much parental concern. Tessa, there are things I have to tell you.''

"There are things I have to tell you, too,'' she said quietly. "But let's eat first. I made this just for you. I had intended to invite you to sample my cuisine after our date last night.''

"Sample your cuisine,'' he repeated, his eyes sparkling.

"Uh-huh. To woo you with chocolate cake.''

He sat beside her and took a big bite, then nodded his approval. "Would've worked, too. Definitely.'' He took another bite.

"You're too easy.''

"Lucky you.''

"You *were* easier than I anticipated. Not that I'm complaining.'' Tessa tucked her feet under her and tried to relax. Her stomach threatened to rebel against the cake.

"Believe me, I have tried to resist you from the minute I saw you step off the bus the day of your interview.''

"Not me. I did everything I could to worm my way into your life.'' She jabbed her fork at the cake, then set it aside. "I knew the second I laid eyes on you—''

"Knew what?''

Tessa pushed herself off the couch and wandered to the front window. No one was standing guard across the street this time. No one was guarding her heart, either. Or Chase's. Nothing could protect them now from the truth. She opened the topic herself.

"Tell me about your childhood, Chase. You said you never knew your father.''

She heard him set his plate on the coffee table. The quiet that followed was filled with the beating of her heart, like a clock ticking off the minutes until a dynamite blast.

"There was a name on my birth certificate, but my mother told me she made it up. Truth was, she didn't know his name. It was a one-night fling. They didn't exchange names.''

She kept her back to him, figuring he'd come to her when he wanted to.

"My mother was an alcoholic for as long as I can remember

Whatever money she earned here and there went toward booze. We lived hand-to-mouth, but I didn't know anything different so it didn't faze me much, until I got older and realized that other kids didn't live like that. When I was about eight I started taking money from my mother's purse and hiding it. I'd pay the rent and buy groceries with what I could stash away. She never noticed.''

Tessa could picture him at eight, his gray eyes far too worldly for a child. ''You had a lot of responsibility.''

''I didn't mind that because it meant we'd be able to stay in one place, and there'd be food on the table. What I hated was how my mother would disappear for days on end. She'd finally show up again, apologetic, usually bringing me a gift of some sort. We'd settle into a routine again, and then off she'd go.''

''What did you do?''

He came up beside her and leaned against the window frame opposite her. ''Went to school. Pretended like nothing was wrong. Never got into any trouble, so that there wouldn't be any reason for the school to contact her.''

Tessa's heart swelled as she looked at him and saw the child again. Stark pain lined his face.

''That's what my life was like—until I was fourteen. She went away again and she never came back.'' He looked out the window. ''I waited. Days. Weeks. A month. No word. No sign of her. To this day I don't know what happened. She just vanished.''

Tears pricked Tessa's eyes. The loneliness must have been unbearable for him. The uncertainty. The fear. ''What did you do?''

''Well, no one would hire me, of course. And every story I'd heard about foster homes led me to believe I didn't want that to be my only option. But my time ran out. The rent was due, and I wasn't eating enough to fuel my body, which was going through a growth spurt. I was desperate, Tessa. Can you understand that?''

''Of course I can,'' she said, extending her hand.

He walked away from her, just far enough that she couldn't touch him, comfort him.

"There was a group of boys who hung around the neighborhood. Today we would call them a gang. Then...I don't know. They were bullies, certainly, and older than me by two or three years. They caught wind of my situation, and they promised to pay my rent if they could use my apartment—and I use the term loosely, because it was smaller than yours—as their hangout. I didn't see how I had any other choice. So, I just kept going to school—I was in eighth grade, almost to the end of the school year. At night I'd stay at the public library until it closed. Then I'd come home and sleep in the bathtub because they were entertaining their girlfriends.

"And then everything changed," he said.

"In what way?"

"They decided I needed to stock my refrigerator. So they took me down to a local market, one of those neighborhood places, you know?"

Tessa nodded.

"They were going to shoplift some food for me. I argued with them. They made all sorts of threats, everything from notifying the police to telling my landlord. I was too scared about what would happen to me, so I did what they asked. They ordered me to stand guard outside the front entrance. I was supposed to prevent anyone from coming in. They didn't care how I managed it."

He ran his fingers through his hair. He glanced at her for a second, then looked away. "I was lucky. No one came along, but they were taking too long to just be grabbing some stuff and running. And then I heard sirens. I didn't know if it was the police, but I used it as an excuse to go into the store and warn the boys off." He looked at the ceiling. "They weren't shoplifting. One of them was holding a gun on the clerk, an eighteen-year-old boy whose eyes were filled with terror like I'd never seen. The others were gathered in a circle watching as one kid raped a girl—a sixteen-year-old girl who'd broken up with him the week before and who was now dating the store clerk. The boys had gone to the store, knowing she'd be there, already knowing what they were going to do. They just hadn't counted on the clerk hitting a silent alarm to the police department.''

He shoved his hands in his pockets.

"I could've gotten away. I could have. But I didn't want the police to hurt the girl, to shoot anyone by mistake. I don't know what I thought I could do to prevent it, though. Everything happened so fast. It's all just a blur of people and shouting and gunshots. When it was over, the clerk had been shot by the kid who'd held him at gunpoint, and the bullet severed his spine, paralyzing him from the waist down. The kid who raped the girl fired at the police and was shot and killed in return fire.''

"And what happened to you?''

"Me?'' He looked in surprise at her. "What does it matter? Someone died. Someone got paralyzed. Some poor girl was raped. I was alive and undamaged.''

"Not undamaged. You've carried this burden ever since. You wouldn't even let yourself have a physical relationship with a woman.''

"Tessa, on those rare occasions I even considered it, I'd look at the woman and see that girl. I'll never forget her face. Never.''

"You made love with me.''

"Which is why I'm telling you my story. You're different. Everything's different. But you have a right to know who I am. Where I came from. What I've done.''

"You were abandoned and bewildered and helpless. You didn't know you had any other choice.''

His hands tightened into fists. "I knew the difference between right and wrong. I knew that the longer they stayed in the store, the more trouble they were getting into. I should have gone in sooner. I should have been brave enough to go in there. Maybe I could have stopped it. Maybe so many lives wouldn't have been destroyed, then.''

"And maybe not.'' She walked up to him. Recognizing that he still didn't want her to touch him, she kept her hands at her

sides. "They had a plan. Do you really think anything you said
or did could have swayed them?"

"I should have tried."

"Chase. Given what you've learned since then, in your life and
in your training, you must realize they probably would have shot
you if you'd interfered."

"Maybe it would have been better than living with it." His
lips compressed into a hard line. "I've worked every day since
then to see that no other child experiences what I did. I've paid
all along. Sacrificed. It never seems to be enough. Nothing I do
seems to be enough. The memory doesn't fade, Tessa. It doesn't
fade.

"Sarge took me in because he saw hope in the fact I'd never
quit going to school. He required a lot of me, and I didn't let him
down."

"He's very proud of you. And you should be proud of yourself
and what you've accomplished. Are you, Chase? Or will no
amount of repayment satisfy you? Doesn't it have to end some
time? You've been your own judge, jury, jailer and executioner.
Even convicted criminals are given a second chance after paying
their debt to society. I haven't met a better person, a better citizen
than you. You've served your sentence."

Chase swept her into his arms. Freedom like he'd never known
raced through him. Light beckoned him toward the end of the
dark, seemingly endless tunnel he'd lived in. He wanted to embrace that light, that new beginning he'd anticipated when he'd
made love to Tessa for the first time, knowing then that she was
going to change his life forever.

Forever. The word resonated in his mind, then meandered
down his body to weave through all the chambers of his heart,
tightening and tugging like a lasso. Did he dare believe his life
could change?

"I know that an experience that traumatic doesn't go away,"
Tessa said. "It stays coiled inside you and it springs up at the

oddest moments. Sometimes you can figure out what triggered the memory, sometimes not.''

''Yes.'' He tipped her head back and kissed her, gently, gratefully. ''I don't want to go home. I don't want to leave you.''

Tessa pressed her face to his shoulder, summoning up enough strength to open the subject she'd been dreading. ''You may change your mind.''

He was a silent a minute. ''I've told you the worst there is to know about me, Tessa. You can do the same. Trust me.''

''I trust you with my life.'' She pushed away from him and took a step back as she gathered her courage. ''Most of what you told me tonight I already knew.''

''How?''

''Because I remember that night, too.''

The fragile foundation of Chase's new world cracked. ''You remember?'' he asked carefully.

She lifted her chin. He saw her lips quiver before she answered, ''The boy who was paralyzed is my brother, Brent. Half brother, actually. My mother's son from her first marriage.''

He took a step back. Then another, and another. His flesh drew taut across his cheeks. His eyes dulled. ''You knew— You knew who I was before you were hired?''

''I took the job *because* I knew who you were. I wanted to get to know you. I hadn't known your name before. My parents protected me from everything that happened in the aftermath of that night. But I found out last month that you've been giving Brent money for years. I needed to know more about the man who would do that.''

A long silence, ominous and thick, blanketed the room. Abruptly, Chase turned away, unable to look at her.

''Our relationship started with a lie.'' The agony of that realization splintered the feelings he'd just started to accept, *to believe he deserved*. ''I hadn't been with a woman before you. Didn't you think that meant anything, Tessa? Didn't you think that it was important? Important enough to tell me the truth before—''

He shoved his hands through his hair. "My God. I haven't lied to anyone since that horrible night, not even the smallest of white lies. You know that about me, if nothing else. By keeping the truth from me, you've mocked everything I value. Everything I am."

He could hardly breathe, thinking about it. There was no place to hide, no one to offer comfort. He couldn't stay here another second, not now. He headed for the door.

"Wait! Chase, please. Just listen for a minute. Please."

"I can't." He twisted the first lock.

"I was there that night, too!"

He stopped and turned. "What?"

She came closer. "I was upstairs. The alarm Brent triggered also rang upstairs. My parents had gone to the movies. It was a school night, so I had to stay home. Brent worked at the store. When all the shooting stopped, I crept down the stairway that connected the store to our apartment. I saw everything. I saw *you*. You were the first person I saw when I peeked into the store, and the last person I saw before a policeman spotted me and took me back upstairs."

The implications of her revelation sank in. Aside from the fact she'd lied to him, there was the stark reality that they never could have had a future. She would have to choose between her family and him. He couldn't ask that of her, even if he wanted to.

He twisted the second lock. He had to get out of there.

She spoke to his back, her words rushed and desperate. "My memory of that night is vivid—the blood that was everywhere, the terrifying sound of the girl's unrelenting sobs, my brother being tended to by paramedics. And your face, Chase. *Your face.* The shock, the agony, the regret. That image stayed with me until the day I walked into your office and saw the adult you, which instantly replaced the adolescent in my head. I never meant any harm. I was fascinated by what you'd done with your life. I admired you even before I met you."

"Then you should have told me the truth."

"You never would have hired me, much less come to care for me. You wouldn't have let yourself."

"That's right."

"Oh, please don't shut down on me. Don't let yourself be filled with ice after all the warmth we've shared."

"False warmth, Tessa. Completely false."

"And what about destiny?"

"What about it?"

"I believe we were meant to be. We've been linked for all these years. Neither of us shared ourselves with anyone else. You said it yourself—it happened so fast. It happened that fast because it was destined to be. I love you, Chase. I kept my secret because I knew you wouldn't ever accept those words from me if you knew everything from the beginning. I don't regret keeping the secret. I only regret that we have to suffer through this before we can find our future together."

Silence filled the space between them, heavy and painful. The not-having had been so much easier to live with than the giving-up. It was the first time he'd heard the words "I love you." If she'd said them without lying to him first, he would have taken them inside him and let them be his guiding light forever. But now he could only deny their truth.

He opened the door and moved into the hall, not looking back at her. "There can't be a future, Miss Rose."

"I'm your destiny," she said so softly he almost didn't hear her.

He stumbled a step, but he kept walking—out of her life, out of the first truly happy time of his existence. He didn't believe in destiny. Destiny didn't lie. Destiny didn't hurt. Destiny didn't crush tender feelings and newly blossomed souls.

Destiny would seek out and match what was right and good and perfect.

No. She wasn't his destiny. She was his final punishment.

# Ten

Tessa decided that if one more person at the Center looked pity-ingly at her she was going to scream. She'd thought she and Chase had been discreet about their relationship, but apparently not. Everyone had noticed the interest, the sparkle, the whatever-kinds-of-signals people who are attracted to each other give off—because everyone noticed that it was gone. So now they tiptoed around her, and probably Chase, as well.

It had been the worst three days of her life. She'd hardly slept. She'd barely eaten enough to keep a mouse alive. But through it all, she remained confident that he would accept fate, as she had.

He didn't seem in a hurry to do so, however. He hadn't spoken a word to her beyond directly-to-the-point business inquiries. She saw him only when he escorted Dodger to the kitchen. He was always out of his office, sometimes even out of the building, when she arrived or departed. A less secure woman might think he was avoiding her.

Tessa smiled at her own sorry joke, then forced herself to take another bite of her peanut butter and jelly sandwich. She sat in one of the short-legged children's chairs in her classroom while her charges napped. She wished she could join them, wished she could sleep until Chase changed his mind. The weekend seemed like a lifetime ago, except that she was aware of her body now in ways she never had been before.

The clatter of wheels against the hardwood floors announced Dodger's arrival. She smiled at him as he pushed his handcart through her room. He winked back, then rolled his eyes. Her gaze shifted to the man who trailed him. Last week Chase would have stayed in the room with her until Dodger left. This week he followed him into the kitchen.

She sighed. How were they supposed to work things out if he wouldn't give her a chance to explain?

She tossed Dodger a bag of cookies as he returned, whistling.

"Thanks, Miss Rose."

"You're welcome. Would you like some, Chase?"

"No, thanks."

Then they were gone. She set her chin in her palm, frowning. Pretty soon her eyes closed. She'd rest for a minute. Just for a minute....

She jerked awake. With a quick glance at the clock she realized she'd slept ten minutes and it was time to get the afternoon's art project together. She gathered up her lunch remains and shoved everything into her thermal sack, then stowed it in her desk.

An hour after she got home that night, she dumped out her lunch bag. She set the extra bag of cookies aside for tomorrow. The rest went into the trash.

Something made her look into her garbage can after she'd tossed the waxed paper and plastic wrap. A crumpled envelope lay on top, beside a baggie containing her half-eaten apple. She plucked the envelope out using metal tongs and set it on her counter, not sure why she was being so careful, but responding to the icy fingers that played a dirge along her spine.

Reacting from gut instinct, she dug out a business card and dialed the pager number listed. A minute later her phone rang.

"This is Inspector O'Keefe."

"Leslie, this is Tessa Rose. I may be overreacting here, but someone left an envelope in my classroom today. There's nothing written on it. It's sealed up, though, and there's a piece of paper inside. I'd drifted to sleep for a few minutes during lunch, so I think someone put it on my table while I was sleeping. It might not be anything at all. One of the kids might have delivered a note from a parent and just didn't want to disturb me while I slept. But something tells me otherwise."

"I'll come over. I want to talk to you, anyway. Don't touch it, please."

Tessa stared at the paper intruder for the fifteen minutes it took for Leslie to arrive. Wearing latex gloves, Leslie slit the envelope open and pulled out the contents, a single sheet with a message of words snipped out of newspaper and magazine print and pasted to the page.

The foul message turned Tessa's stomach. Along with the revulsion came fear—and determination not to let it send her cowering.

"This confirms that your assault wasn't random, after all," Leslie said. "He'd definitely targeted you."

"I can see that. Now what?"

Leslie dropped the letter and envelope into a large baggie and sealed it shut. "I'll have it analyzed. Sometimes we can get a handle on people by the magazine print. Many use distinctive type styles that we can trace, and then the magazine itself becomes a lead."

"But I don't have any enemies, as far as I know. I've lived a quiet life, without any kind of unusual attention. Why would anyone want to harm me?"

"It isn't a coincidence that this began after you moved here. It's probably someone new in your life, maybe someone you haven't even met but who sees you around. Obviously someone who's aware of where you work and who you spend time with. Who is he referring to as your fellow fornicator?''

Tessa met Leslie's direct gaze. "Chase."

"Are you sure?"

"Well, he's been the only man I've...had a relationship with." She linked her fingers, feeling the sweat that glued her palms together.

"Have you stayed overnight with each other?"

"Yes. Here, last week, the night of the assault. He slept on the cushions on the floor. Then last weekend I stayed with him."

Leslie stood. "I'll give Chase a call. He can come—"

"He won't. He's really mad at me." Tessa bounced her legs, embarrassed at having to reveal so much to a close friend of Chase. "At this point, I could drop off the face of the earth and he wouldn't care."

"If you can say that, you don't know a thing about Chase Ryan." Leslie dialed. "Hi, it's Les. Listen, we've got a bit of a problem."

Revolted, Chase hurled the baggie back at Leslie. "This scum better hope you catch him before I do."

"Don't mess with the evidence, Chase. And stay out of it. The investigation will intensify now. But you can see that you're potentially a target for this bastard, too, Chase, not just Tessa. He's angry. He's possessive. He believes he can protect her from you. That's enough reason to lie low."

"I'm not sitting on my butt doing nothing."

"I didn't hear that." She stared at him for several seconds. "Now, something I want to talk to you both about. Tessa, you said you rammed your fingers into this guy's eyes, right?"

"Through the holes in the ski mask. I definitely got him."

"Do you think you scratched him with your fingernails?"

Chase looked directly at Tessa for the first time since he'd walked in the door. She was calm, controlled, but...fragile. She looked like she'd gotten about as much sleep as he had.

"I don't know, Leslie. I hurt him. He covered his eyes with his hands. That's when I got away. Why?"

"Well, the kid, Bobby, didn't have any sign of injury around his eyes the next day. What about—" She looked at Chase and stopped.

"Tell her, Les. She deserves to know."

"Know what?" Tessa asked.

"Dodger has a record of assault against women. Three arrests, one conviction. He served some time for battery."

"You think Dodger is doing this? No. He likes me. I give him cookies!" She met Chase's gaze and held up a hand, palm out. "That was stupid, I suppose. It's just that I always thought I had good instincts about people."

"He's stayed out of trouble since he spent some time in jail. But you need to be careful," Leslie said. "Did you notice any problem with his eyes? Chase, did you?"

Tessa shook her head. "He winked at me today. He was fine."

"Last week, though?"

Chase pictured the wiry young man. "He wore his baseball cap differently. Usually he wears it backwards. Not last week."

"Did he avoid your gaze? Tessa, did he wink at you then?"

"I don't know," they said simultaneously.

"It seems like he always winks at me," Tessa added. "I can't be sure."

Leslie closed her notebook and dropped it into her pocket. "If you think of anything else, give me a call. Now, what are we going to do about you, Tessa? I don't think you should be staying here alone. Do you have a friend who'll move in? Could you go back to your parents' house for a while?"

"She can stay with me." Chase didn't glance her way. He kept his focus on Leslie as she stood and walked to the door.

"Good. Tessa, you keep him out of trouble, okay?"

"Okay." Her voice was barely above a whisper.

When the door shut behind Leslie, Chase finally met Tessa's

gaze. "You'll need to pack a couple of bags so that you don't have to come back here too soon."

"You don't have to do this."

"Yes, I do, Tessa. I think this is the last thing I have to do. And then I'll be free. Full circle."

"But a full circle brings you back to the beginning. And I was there, then, too. No matter where you stop along the way, it's always going to lead to me."

He shoved his hands in his pockets. "Maybe my analogy was wrong, but you get my point."

She was quiet a long time. "I miss your smile," she said sadly, then she turned away to gather her things.

Her woman's touch was evident almost immediately in his austere apartment. Her clothes hung beside his in the bedroom closet. Cosmetics took up a square foot of space on his bathroom vanity. Her shampoo sat beside his in the shower, the bottles touching, her way of reminding him of what they'd shared, he was sure.

He'd cleared an entire dresser drawer just so that her undergarments wouldn't mingle with his, so he couldn't stroke the silky fabric or picture the garment hugging her body. He'd watched her pack everything and was a little surprised by her panties and bras, wildly colorful and temptingly sheer. Part of the whole feminine package, he decided, along with the long, curly hair and the ultrafeminine clothing she favored. He'd seen her in jeans only once.

Chase glanced at his bedside clock—2:00 a.m. They'd gone to bed almost two hours ago. Tessa had insisted on sleeping on the couch, even though he had to get up hours before she did and he would undoubtedly make enough noise to wake her. Stretched out on his bed now, his arms folded behind his head, he gave up any pretense of trying to sleep. He probably should just read, but he couldn't imagine anything holding his interest.

A whisper of sound penetrated the night. Tessa. She stood in his open doorway, illuminated just enough from the night-light in the hall that he could see she was wearing something long and pale. He shut his eyes and rolled to his side, not wanting to talk to her. Not in the middle of the night, in a room filled with memories. She'd deceived him. She couldn't just waltz back into his life and expect things to be the same.

She didn't enter his room, though. He heard the bathroom door shut, then water running. Not from the sink. She was filling the tub.

He sat up, then leaned his elbows against his upraised knees and rested his head in his hands. The link she talked about between them, the bond, had been rooted in a violent act, then lay dormant for years and now was blossoming out of violence again. Someone's obsession. Someone who didn't see the gentleness in her, who saw only her sexuality. Obviously someone who didn't know her as a person, but as an object.

He straightened. Okay. That was a good place to start. Now, who were the potential suspects? Bobby Moran. Underneath that bravado he respected Tessa, respected her for protecting herself well against him and even more so for how she handled her attacker. Chase eliminated Bobby from the list.

Dodger. An obvious suspect, given his past. The opportunity was there, too. However, Chase couldn't ignore the fact that Dodger did seem to genuinely like Tessa. Except that Chase had also caught the young man eyeing her blatantly—and he hadn't been smiling or winking then.

Who else had she met since she started working here? He ran a mental list of the people at the Center and came up empty. What about at her apartment house? There was Norm—who had a girlfriend. He'd have to ask Tessa about the other tenants.

He considered the shops between the Center and her apartment. A liquor store, dry cleaner, several restaurants. Video rentals. Bookstore. Too many people who could see her come and go.

His thoughts kept returning to the attack itself. She hadn't been out that early in the morning before. Who would have expected it? Who could have caught wind of it? Or was *that* attack random, as Leslie first believed, but was now focused. The attacker had found out *since then* who she was and wanted retribution.

This was starting to make sense, and simplified his plan to discover the man's identity. Chase could use himself as bait. Someone hadn't protected that other poor girl all those years ago. He wouldn't leave Tessa open to the same fate.

He heard the bathroom door open, surprising him. She'd just turned off the water. Why wasn't she up to her chin in bubbles?

"Tessa?" he called out quietly.

She stopped in his doorway.

"Are you all right?"

"I'm fine. 'Night."

There was something in her voice, though. "Could you come here a minute?"

She came in but stopped a couple of feet from his bed.

"What's wrong?" he asked.

"Nothing."

He moved over, opening up space beside him on the bed. "Sit down, please."

She perched on the edge of the bed.

"Can't sleep?"

She shook her head.

"Thought a hot bath would help?"

She shrugged.

He wrapped a hand around her wrist. She was cold, not warm and dewy as if straight from a bath.

"I changed my mind," she said defensively.

He waited.

"All right," she said finally, harshly. "All right. I didn't want you to hear me crying, so I ran water to cover the sound. Okay? Is that all right with you if I tried to be considerate?"

"Why were you crying?"

"Oh, no reason. No reason at all." She folded her arms across her chest. "Just because I finally became independent and now I'm a prisoner. And because I have to lie to my parents." Her voice caught. "And because I'm scared, and you hate me, and I don't know how I screwed up so much all at one time."

He could see her hold back tears, and his throat constricted in response.

"I'm sorry, Chase. I'm sorry for all the pain and all the problems I've brought to your life. But I know that you're mine and I'm yours and nothing short of death is going to change that. And I know you don't want to hear it. But I love you. You can't ignore that forever. Good night."

No, he couldn't ignore it forever. But, for now, he had to.

Because Chase specifically instructed Tessa not to become his housekeeper, Tessa vacuumed on Saturday morning, feeling smug at disobeying his direct order. That man was entirely too self-sufficient. He didn't even want her to earn her keep while she lived with him. Ha! Little did he know about her. She could be just as stubborn as he. And she wasn't about to be waited on as well as guarded. What did he think, that she was some hothouse flower who would wilt if her fingers touched scouring powder?

Idiot. More than a little irritated now, Tessa yanked the plug when she'd vacuumed as far as she could, given the length of the cord, then switched to another electrical outlet. She moved into the bedroom and attacked the carpet in there as she thought about the past few days.

They coexisted. She didn't know any other way of defining their relationship. They didn't argue. They didn't tease each other. They shared space and, occasionally, meals. Sometimes late at night he'd sit at the kitchen counter with her and cut construction paper into pieces for the next day's art project, but they didn't talk about anything personal, even though she'd tried at first, then gave up when she was greeted with stony silence. Really, it was all becoming tedious—and rather childish.

In one sense she understood. He'd held off becoming intimate until the relationship was singularly important—the same as she had, she'd like to remind him—and then things hadn't turned out as perfectly as he'd expected. Perfection was just a word, and certainly didn't apply to Tessa or their relationship. Or any relationship, for that matter. But his ideals were tarnished now, and all the polishing and buffing in the world weren't going to make those ideals shine again. Virginity could only be lost—given— once, after all, but the experience should effect a beginning, not an end.

Tessa picked up a pair of his shoes so that she could vacuum under them, continuing to dissect their relationship. Living with him should have been easy, but it was impossible. She was an *obligation*. She didn't want to be anyone's obligation.

She shoved the vacuum brush under his bed. Actually, there was little dust anywhere. He hardly spent enough time in the apartment to bring in dirt, and he'd developed the habit of cleaning as he went. He'd make some woman a good husband someday.

She sighed, then tried to distract herself. It didn't work. She wanted to kiss him so much her mouth hurt from thinking about it.

He didn't think she had good self-restraint, but he didn't know how often she'd dug her fingernails into her palms so that she wouldn't touch him. She wanted to soothe the tension from his face. She wished she could run her hands along his body. She needed to feel the definition of muscle across his broad chest and strong shoulders, and down his back. She'd give anything to watch him walk across the room one more time, naked and taut and powerful. She relived dancing with him, smiled at his surprise at having two climaxes so close together, marveled at her own incredible sense of fulfillment each time they'd made love.

She wanted to see him smile again. To hear him laugh. He'd only laughed once, but she hadn't forgotten the sound.

Well. So much for distracting herself.

Exchanging the carpet tool for the dusting brush, she started in on the bookshelves. Floor-to-ceiling, wall-to-wall books. Books about psychology and plumbing repair and faraway lands. Best-selling fiction, Chaucer, Twain. And—

Tessa slid a paperback off the shelf. A big fat historical romance novel? With a smile she tucked the vacuum hose under her arm, opened the book to a dog-eared page—and found a love scene. A spicy, steamy, oh-please-let-me-exchange-places-with-that-woman love scene.

Memories flooded Tessa as she read. Yes, the author had done a good job of capturing the emotions, the sensations, the oblivion.

She reread the scene, then found another turned-down page. Another passionate moment, another satisfied hero and—

"What are you doing?"

Tessa jumped at the sound of Chase's voice, which accompanied the abrupt loss of sound from the vacuum. Heat roared through her, from her face to her feet. "Um. Reading?" When he scowled deeper, she wrapped herself up in a shawl of bravado. "No wonder you were able to 'muddle through' so well," she said pertly, reminding him of his own words before they made love the first time.

Chase carefully pulled the book out of her hand, although he'd been inclined to snatch it away.

She smiled. "I think you did some of those things to me...."

He studied her—the challenging eyes and flickering smile and defensive posture. "I didn't buy that book," he said.

Her smile broadened.

"It was left downstairs. When no one claimed it, I brought it up here and put it on my shelf in case someone asked eventually."

"Uh-huh."

"I don't lie."

"So you've said. I didn't hear anything about not reading it, however, Chase."

He returned the book to its alphabetical place. "I read everything."

"Did you enjoy it?"

"I don't remember."

She made a sound that strongly suggested she didn't believe him. He'd never heard anyone actually snicker before, but he was pretty sure that the sound she made could be called snickering.

"All right," he said, taking the vacuum hose from her. "It held my interest. And why are you cleaning when I asked you not to?"

"What would you like the prisoner to do, Warden? There isn't an automobile-license-making machine in sight. Anyway, I'm done. All I have left is grocery shopping and a trip home to pick up mail."

"Les is going to stop by. You can give her your key and she'll pick up your mail. It's not safe for you to go home."

"We haven't heard anything for days," she said, frustration heavy in her voice. "If you're with me, I don't see why I can't—"

He plucked something from his back pocket and thrust it at her. "This time he sent a letter to me."

Chase was furious. The missive was similar to Tessa's in that it contained cut-up letters pasted on a piece of paper, and the words were just as repulsive, but what stung the most was the implication that he didn't deserve Tessa.

Like he didn't already know that? He'd known since they met. He'd just forgotten it temporarily when his hormones decided to make a jailbreak. He'd been trying to keep the fugitives under control ever since, but they had ideas of their own and had been steadily digging another tunnel toward freedom.

"Chase."

"Don't let it break your spirit," he said, hearing something new in her voice—defeat.

"I can't deal with this." She sat on the edge of his bed, her head bent. "I thought I could. But I don't deserve what he's doing to me. Neither do you."

He almost touched her hair. He almost buried his face in it. But if he had, he wouldn't have stopped there. He'd never had anyone to care for before, not like this.

And her family would never accept him.

She looked up. Her eyes beseeched him. "Ever since you brought me here I've been trying to talk to you about...things. I need for you to listen."

He walked away from her and stood staring at his books. For years they'd brought him information and pleasure—and companionship. People and problems surrounded him sixteen hours a day. Books took him out of that world for a while.

He hadn't read since she'd come to stay with him. His concentration was shot, his interest nil. A whole new world had been opened to him last weekend, one of light and joy and carnal pleasure beyond anything he'd expected. The books hadn't exaggerated about that. He didn't want to retreat into that old, dark existence again. He just didn't see that he had a choice.

Tomorrow he'd start trying to flush their enemy out of hiding. Tomorrow he'd try to lure the scorpion out from under his rock. Tomorrow.

But today—

"As soon as Les leaves," he said, turning toward Tessa, "why don't we go for a drive, maybe have a picnic. I'll listen to whatever you have to say."

"Thank you."

Thank *you,* he thought. For everything you've given me. Because even as painful as this is now, it really is better to have loved and lost, than never to have loved at all.

# Eleven

If their situation had been different, Chase would have taken Tessa to Sebastian's hideaway in the Sierra Nevada mountains. They could have spread out a blanket under the canopy of trees behind the cabin. He would have teased her out of her clothing, convinced her not to be shy about being outdoors and naked. The property was isolated, and their chances of being discovered negligible. They could have fed each other delicacies from their picnic stash, then fed other demanding needs.

Instead, he settled for a rocky bluff overlooking the Pacific, north of San Francisco. They hiked down a trail to the beach and sat within a jut carved by thousands of years of ocean pounding against rock, and were well shielded from the elements. They weren't entirely alone. Occasionally someone would walk by, but no one paid them particular attention.

Chase watched her as he finished his lunch. Her hair lifted with the breeze as she stared at the ocean, her chin resting on her knees. She sifted sand with her fingers.

"I haven't gotten away like this in years," she said. "I forgot how peaceful the ocean can be."

"If I had a choice," he said, scanning the horizon, "I'd have a house overlooking the ocean. With more beach than this, though. More sand."

"I'd like to go to Hawaii."

The wistful tone made him look at her. She leaned back on her hands and stretched out her legs. Where her blouse gapped a little, he could see enough of the dark blue bra hugging her flesh to tease him into a response he didn't want, but couldn't seem to fight. He drew up his knee and let the reaction happen. She couldn't see, anyway. Wouldn't know.

She didn't seem to be in a hurry to talk, which was fine with him. It'd been a long time since he'd taken a Saturday off, and he felt like a balloon with a slow leak.

He followed the movement of her hand as she unbuttoned her blouse and slid it off. Not a bra underneath but a bathing suit.

Suddenly nothing else seemed to matter, not promises he'd made to himself or statements he'd made to her. He didn't care that he couldn't have her. He didn't care that someone intended them harm. He only wanted to enjoy her and this time together.

"Using all your available weapons, I see," he said, resigned.

She smiled. "I was warm."

"Right. That's why you've got goose bumps all down your arms, and your nipples are hard."

"Do you want me to put my blouse back on?"

"No." The word came out more violently than he'd intended.

"Maybe I should take off my shorts, too."

The not-so-innocent look she gave him sent bolts of lightning straight into his loins.

"Go ahead."

Tessa heard the challenge in his voice. Go on. Torture me. Tease me. See how strong I can be. See how well I can resist temptation.

The problem was, she really didn't want to know how well he could resist.

"I've missed you," she said, resting her cheek on her upraised knees and looking at him. "I can't believe how quickly I felt comfortable with you. You made it so easy last weekend, Chase. So right."

"Sometimes I wasn't sure of that. I was afraid I was coming on too strong."

"No. Whatever awkwardness or shyness I had came from first-time jitters. I've never been happier."

"I felt the same."

His need for honesty obviously outweighed his need to keep her at a distance, Tessa thought. Otherwise he wouldn't have given her hope with his words.

"But it doesn't change anything, Tessa."

The barrier landed with a thud between them.

"No, I guess it doesn't. So maybe I should just tell you about my brother, and the experience, and how our lives changed because of it." She pulled her blouse back on, although she didn't button it. "I'd never even heard the word *rape* until that night. I had a vague idea of what sex was, but, at eleven, I was still pretty innocent. I thought sex was something that happened only so that babies could be born.

"Brent and I are seven years apart in age. We didn't have a lot in common because of that, of course, but I loved and admired him, as little sisters do. We didn't use the term half brother or half sister, ever. Brent's father had died when he was four, and my dad raised him as his own, although he never adopted him or changed his name because my mother wanted Brent's family name to continue. We didn't have much, but we were happy."

She raked her fingers through the sand as the memories filtered in. "Everything changed that night. Everything. I grew up overnight. Brent's life stopped. My mom clung to me. My dad became so strict, so obsessed with safety—I can't tell you how obsessed, even now. He sold the store and we moved to a different part of the city where I could attend a new school. Brent's name had been in the newspaper but not ours, so no one knew who I was. I wasn't allowed to talk about it with anyone. I had to pretend it hadn't happened. Yet, there was Brent, in a wheelchair, needing attention and care. And I became as much a prisoner as he was. I never even had a date until I was in college.''

Chase watched her expression. Dispassionate. Unemotional. Accepting. ''I'm sorry.''

That triggered a strong response, and he was fascinated by the changes that made her eyes glitter and her mouth harden.

''Don't say that. You have nothing to be sorry for, Chase. Nothing. You were a victim, just like Brent. It wasn't your fault. When will you be able to see that?''

''We'll never agree on that, I guess. I knew right from wrong, even then. I knew.''

''I thought we'd decided that you had paid your debt.''

''This is not a debt that can be easily erased, Tessa. Believe me, I've tried.''

''How can you ever erase it if you continue to give Brent money every month?''

He heard the accusation in her voice. ''You're criticizing me for helping to provide for your brother?''

''Yes!''

''Why?''

''Because not only did it keep the event constantly alive for you, it also held Brent back. Because you had the best of intentions but got the worst of results. With all your education and practical experience, you never saw that you were enabling him to do nothing, instead of being productive?''

Chase sat speechless. He'd never thought—

''It was hard for Brent. Almost impossible. He was a star athlete, and suddenly he couldn't even walk. But eventually he came to some level of acceptance. He started college to learn about computers. After his first semester, he decided he didn't want to go anymore. He retreated into a television world—except for the first Sunday of every month, when he'd make my mother take him to a little park in the old neighborhood, rain or shine, and leave him there while she was in church. It was the only time he left the house other than for doctor's appointments."

"I always meet him there," Chase said. "I had to make restitution, Tessa. Can't you see that? I had to. He wasn't able to work. In the beginning I could only afford a small amount, but the amount has grown as my income has increased. I don't need much. Why shouldn't I share it with someone who does need it?"

"But Brent *was* able to work. He *chose* not to. I know you see it as a point of honor." She turned to face him fully, tucking her legs under her and leaning forward. "But that's not what the outcome was."

Shock held him immobile for a long time. "I didn't know. I didn't realize," he said at last.

He looked away from her. The sound of the waves no longer soothed him. The salty tang in the air no longer made him wish for a home of his own where he could see the crabs skitter at the shoreline and hear the gulls call. And his children play in the surf. And Tessa— No. That picture had to be destroyed.

He swiped a hand down his face. "I saw him on campus when I first started college. I recognized him. How could I forget? I'd searched for him once before, without luck. I was glad, because I could do something tangible, finally."

"Chase, you've been doing something tangible ever since that night. You keep yourself shut off emotionally, and *still* people admire you, defend you, *care about you*. No child should have to grow up as fast as you did, but you turned out better than okay." She wrapped a hand around his wrist. "You can't take on the whole world's problems. No one can. Not even a superhuman like you."

Despair flowed into him. The value of everything he was, everything he'd sought to do, faded. "I'm not superhuman. I've just been trying to do the right thing."

"I know." Her eyes pleaded with him. "I do understand your intentions were honorable."

"But 'the road to hell is paved with good intentions,'" he said, feeling the burden settle fully on his shoulders.

"Not hell. Not for you." Tessa scooted close to him. "There's a special place in heaven waiting for you. But it's your life on earth that you need to think about now. I don't mean to tell you what to do. You'll make your own decisions. I just thought that you should know about Brent. When I found out last month that he'd been accepting money from you, and then learned who you were, I was compelled to meet you, to see what made you tick. I never expected to fall in love with you. But I did. And I'm not sorry about it. You're entitled to a whole life, Chase, not just the safe world you've created."

His frown deepened. "Safe? My life was threatened today by someone who is too much of a coward to face me directly. Your life—"

"Your life has been completely safe—emotionally. Oh, you care about people. Sarge. Leslie. Ben and Gabe and Sebastian. Everyone who comes to the Center and all those children you still hope to save. But your heart has never been in danger before."

"You think my heart is in danger now?"

Tessa felt the sting of tears at his self-protective response. She laid a hand against his face, ran her thumb across his unyielding lips. "I hope so. I love you so much."

Everything inside Chase heated up, threatening a meltdown of every barrier he'd erected. She'd said the words before, but there was something different about the way she said them this time. Something magical and hopeful and reassuring. Something pure and clean and new. Something necessary.

"I know you're angry with me for not telling you who I was when I first came to the Center," she said softly, "but I'm not sorry. Please don't hate me for it."

He didn't know what to do. She thought the lie stood between them. He could deal with the lie—had already dealt with it. He

understood her reasoning. But her family. He couldn't come between her and her family, which was what would have to happen.
The wheelchair was her brother's constant reminder. Her mother
worried. Her father had sold his business, moved them away to
safer ground. Anonymous territory.

How likely was he to forgive Chase his part in the huge
changes in their lives? Lifelong changes. If they didn't hold a
grudge against him, they would be saints.

And yet...and yet Tessa sat there like some glorious reward for
every good thing he'd done in his life since then. How could his
reward be Tessa? How could it? But he wanted it to be her.
Needed it.

"I don't hate you," he said, the words scraping his throat.

She smiled, although her eyes still held sadness. "Well. That's
progress, I think."

He pulled her into his arms, tucking her head under his chin.

"How can anything so wonderful hurt so much?" she asked.

He lay back, pulling her with him, tightening his hold as she
threw a leg over his so that she could burrow closer.

Her fingers brushed the hair above his navel. Reaction came
hard and fast and fierce. He moved her blouse aside to stroke the
bare skin of her abdomen. Her fragrant hair teased his nostrils
with a fresh floral scent, her gentle breath whispered encouragement against his neck, her tiny whimper reverberated in his head
like cymbals clanging.

He angled to his side more, covered her with her blouse again,
then slipped a hand under her suit. His palm burned with the feel
of her, taut and tempting. Her eyes closed, her lips parted, ex-
pelling short little breaths.

She glided a knee up to press against his erection, and he
sucked in air, quick and hard.

"Did I tell you how much I loved seeing you nude?" she
asked, opening her eyes and locking gazes with him as she rotated
her knee gently, slowly. "I hadn't realized how strong you are,
how powerful your body is. I wouldn't ever tire of seeing you or

touching you. I can't begin to describe how I feel when I run my hands all over you and your muscles bunch up in response. Or when I wrap my hand around you. Here. Where you're so hot. So velvety soft and yet like iron underneath. And when you're inside me, I burn.''

"Tessa." Her name came out as more of a groan.

"I want to taste you...there. I should have before. I almost did, once. We were in the shower. I've always heard that men couldn't, you know, do it so soon after, but you were getting hard again, even though we'd just... I wanted to—''

Her eyes glittered; her cheeks stained pink. He knew how much she was risking by talking to him this way, but he couldn't stop her. Didn't want to stop her. He needed to know how she felt and what she wanted.

"I wanted to feel the changes," she said, her voice turning husky. She touched a finger to her lips. "Here."

Her words alone took him high. Electrically charged particles gathered low in his body, sizzling and smoldering in a signal he recognized and welcomed. It wouldn't take much to send him over the edge.

She inched closer. "And I wanted you to...you know...to do it to me, too."

His breath whistled through his clamped teeth as she moved her knee lower, sliding her hand between them to shroud him. He clamped his hand around her wrist so his control would not unleash itself and spill free. His pulse pounded there, fast, steady, powerful, as rhythmic as the act itself.

"I wanted to love you with my mouth, too," he said, remembering all the times he'd stopped himself. "I didn't know if it was too soon. I didn't want to rush you."

"What would you have done? Tell me how you would have done it."

Her breathless voice invited him into her fantasy. He moved her hand to touch her own breast. "Feel what I feel," he said, urgency straining his voice. "You're so womanly. Firm and full and soft. Comforting—although I don't think I can explain that, exactly.'' She resisted. He gentled his voice. ''Don't be embarrassed. I wish you could know how just touching you excites me. I liked when you straddled me and leaned over so that I could take your nipple in my mouth and let your breasts overflow in my hands.''

She moaned his name, drawing it out.

He knew she was as aroused as he now. ''You want to know what I would have done to you, Tessa? I would have savored you.''

''How?'' she panted.

How graphic could he get? She couldn't even seem to come up with euphemisms for what they did, what she wanted. In his head he knew exactly what he would have done, where he would have touched. How he would have stroked. How he would have made every fantasy of his—and hers, he hoped—come true. Would saying the words aloud sound crude to her? To him the image and scent of her, so distinctly female, was beautiful. But he was a man.

Laughter floated toward them, forcing them apart hastily. A couple of teenage boys jogged along the shoreline, tossing a Frisbee to a dog that splashed in the surf after he caught it, then bounded up to the boys so the game could begin anew.

Tessa watched them, knowing their arrival had effectively dumped a bucket of ice water on Chase. The fantasy had ended. Her opportunity was lost. She only had to take one quick glance his way to see him retreat—physically, but also emotionally. She tugged her clothing into place.

Now, what should she do? She craved him. If he'd touched her just once she would have found momentary satisfaction then and there. And he was still hard. He couldn't hide that from her. But she knew by the distant look in his eyes that nothing more was going to happen between them.

She tried to understand his personal code of ethics, and decided he was so used to denying himself pleasure that he could ignore the opportunities at will, retreating to someplace inside himself. Someplace where denial reigned supreme and nothing and no one could knock down the fortress he'd built.

"We should get back," he said, scanning the horizon.

Suddenly she didn't want him to be so serious anymore. What had drawn him to her in the first place was that she teased him and flirted with him—and he'd let her. She wanted to recapture the playful beginning of their relationship again. And she thought he needed that, too.

"Why should we get back?" She stood, stripped off her blouse and shorts and headed for the ocean, knowing he was probably focusing on her rear end as she plodded through the sand, intentionally swaying her hips. "I'm going swimming."

"You'll freeze your charming butt."

She turned around and walked backward. "Which is exactly what I need at the moment. Don't you?"

The teenagers were long gone. Once again she and Chase were alone in their little world, with just the ocean and the gulls. She could see him think it over.

"No bathing suit," he said at last, sounding pleased to have come up with an excuse.

She clucked like a chicken, stopping mid-cluck when a wave washed her feet. The water was cold. Really, really cold. Freezing. Whoever thought the Pacific Ocean was warm had never visited northern California. But she wasn't going to let him think she was some cotton candy woman. She clucked again, tucking her hands into her armpits and flapping away.

"What do you expect me to do? Swim naked?" he called out.

"If you want. Or in your skivvies." She grinned at him, pure dare in her eyes.

A great debate was being waged in his head. She could see him weigh the issue. Finally he tugged off his shoes and socks, then rolled up the legs of his jeans almost to his knees. He pulled his shirt over his head, tossing it behind him as he walked toward her. She backed up until she was knee-deep in the water.

Tessa sighed, loving the gift he offered of his naked chest with its sprinkling of dark hair and sculpted muscles, the flat abdomen and that tempting arrow of hair that disappeared into his jeans.

"Do you have any idea how beautiful you are?" he asked.

Startled, she looked at his face, his dear, serious face. "I'm not beautiful. But I'm glad you think so."

"You're like some fairy sprite come to tempt me into a world I didn't know existed outside of books."

Her breath caught at his sincerity. "I'm hardly a sprite. I'm big-boned and not the least dainty. It would take a powerful set of wings for me to take flight."

"I can lift you—" he snapped his fingers "—like that."

"Can not."

"Can, too." He moved in on her, scooped her up and tipped her toward him, so that their lips almost touched. Then he dropped her.

She came up sputtering and yelling, her hair clinging to her body. Her *frozen* body. "Why, you...you— You planned that! You wanted to freeze me out, so you tricked me. Seduced me into letting you pick me up."

Humor lit his eyes. It was worth it, she decided. Worth everything. Anything. Just to see the seriousness in his eyes fade.

"Maybe," he said. "But I only told you the truth."

Tessa lunged, encircling his neck with her arms and his waist with her legs, sharing her cold, wet body with him. He gripped her thighs, holding her in position, then he smiled. He smiled! And then he kissed her, his lips staying curved for the first few seconds, then his tongue invading and dueling with hers.

"Salty," he murmured. "Blends with your peppery mouth."

"Is that a compliment?"

He nuzzled her temple. "Yes."

"You're going to get a hernia if you don't put me down. But don't drop me!" she added in a hurry.

He let go of her legs, keeping his hands at her waist until she found her balance and stepped back. "You know you're going to itch all the way home, with all that salt and sand in your bathing suit.''

She tipped her head to one side, gathered her hair and wrung it out. ''Which I'm sure you were aware of when you dunked me. I'll just take the suit off.''

He raised his brows. ''Without a shower—''

''I know. But it's better than nothing. Come on. You can hold the towel in case someone comes along.''

Chase took her hand and walked with her. He saw her look at their joined hands, then at his face. It was wrong to mislead her like this. Nothing permanent could come of this relationship. Nothing. But nothing in his life had ever felt this good, either. If he was only going to be left with a memory, it should be the best memory possible. So that he would know it hadn't been a dream, but something real and tangible.

They moved close to the rocks, well into the shadows. She didn't seem to expect him to turn around, so he held the towel in front of her but watched her strip. Sand decorated her flesh.

''Want to brush it off?'' she asked, standing still and exposed, only her quickening breath giving away her feelings.

''I want to watch *you* brush it off.''

''You're really into that, aren't you?''

''Into what?''

''Watching me touch myself. That's some kind of turn-on for you.''

''I won't deny that. I've been storing up fantasies for a long time. But mostly I'm just afraid that if I touch you, I won't be able to stop. So it's better if I just watch.''

''And when we get home? What then, Chase?''

''You take a shower.''

''Will you join me?''

He sought reasons why he shouldn't. They were there, just waiting for him to say them aloud. He hesitated so long that she finally seemed to give up on him and started brushing the sand down her, taking her time, turning it into a seduction.

"Will you join me?" she repeated, a different meaning resounding in her tone of voice.

"Maybe."

"The last honest man on earth," she said with a sigh, pulling her shorts over her hips, then slipping into her blouse. "And a man who really knows the meaning of anticipation."

"I seem to be a natural, don't I?"

She traced a salty, sandy finger across his lips, making him realize he was smiling at her.

"You're a natural, all right, Mr. Ryan. And now that you've tasted paradise, are you going to be able to give it up?"

He turned from her, snapping the towel, then folding it. "I don't have a choice."

# Twelve

Sarge glared at Chase. "I'm getting tired of hearing what's going on in your life through Leslie, son."

He'd been waiting at the Center when Chase and Tessa arrived home, and he'd invited himself upstairs. He couldn't have helped but notice the feminine additions in the apartment—a dress draped over a chair back. Fresh flowers in a vase on the coffee table. The pump bottle of hand lotion on the kitchen counter.

"I'm handling it," Chase said.

Tessa was in the shower, having made a beeline to the bathroom the minute they'd walked through the front door.

"I respected your wishes when you asked me to stop following Tessa," Sarge said. "But the notes, Chase, the notes! That changes everything. That's personal. There's no doubt of it now."

"Which is why Tessa has moved in with me, so that she's safe."

"In the meantime you're prisoners. Both of you."

"Not me." Chase walked away from the man he considered a

father, wishing Les had left well enough alone. If he'd wanted Sarge to know, he would've told him. He grabbed a pitcher of iced tea from the refrigerator, offering some to Sarge, as well.

"What does that mean, not you?" Sarge sat at the counter and accepted the glass.

"It means I haven't let the threat handcuff me."

Sarge stared at the Formica countertop and rubbed his forehead. "Why doesn't that surprise me? I s'pose you've got some lame-brain idea of tracking this guy down yourself."

Chase took a long swallow of his drink, then set the glass down carefully. "If I did, I don't s'pose I'd be telling you, would I?"

They did battle with their eyes.

"I saw the notes, son. This is no idle threat."

"I'm aware of that."

Sarge studied him. After a minute he stood, his back a little straighter than usual. "How're the letters being delivered to you?"

"Les canvassed all the kids. She was able to determine that both times someone gave an envelope to a child about to enter the building, along with instructions on who to give it to."

"Description?"

"The first time, a teenage boy with long dark hair. The second time, a girl, maybe ten or so. Les figures someone paid them to bring the letters to the Center."

"Not much to go on."

"Nope."

Sarge wandered away, then looked out the window. "Things are serious with you and Miss Rose."

"I would die for her."

As Sarge turned around, Chase reacted to the statement himself. His heart thumped against his sternum. He was light-headed, thunderstruck, then, finally, focused. He had a purpose now.

"Is it going to come to that?" the older man asked, his voice quavering.

"I don't know. Hope not."

Silence blanketed the room, except for the sound of the shower running.

"She always stay in there that long?" Sarge asked, but clearly wanting to say something else.

"When she shampoos." Chase waited him out. He'd say what he wanted to say, in his own time.

"She know about your past? You know about hers?"

"Meaning what?"

"Meaning nothing but what the questions ask, son."

Chase tried to get a handle on the purpose of the queries. "She knows. I know."

"Are you sure?"

Suspicion stirred like a storm-tossed ship in Chase's stomach. "Do you know about her, Sarge? Do you know of her past? Of our...link?" He paused, reading the answer in Sarge's eyes. "You knew. You didn't tell me."

"It was for her to tell, not me."

Chase took a mental step back. Virgin emotions had been tapped too many times in the past few weeks, but the loss of this particular innocence was almost the most painful. "I always figured your first loyalty would be to me," he said wearily. "I think you should leave."

Sarge moved slowly, looking uncharacteristically frail. Chase didn't weaken.

"You said you would die for her," Sarge intoned, his hand on the doorknob. "But would you kill for her?" He paused. "If it meant guarding her life?"

The shower water stopped. Chase angled that direction, picturing her, naked, clean, pure. Innocent. A woman meant to raise babies and love a man for his whole life. But not him. Not him. His cards had been dealt a long, long time ago. He'd only been bluffing lately, winning a couple of rounds, but not the game.

And never the queen of hearts.

When he turned around, Sarge was gone. And Chase was left

with the big question echoing in his mind. Would he kill for her? Could he?

The scent of her reached him first. Fresh. Fragrant. Tessa. Then the bare whisper of her touch as she ran her fingers along his arm, which tensed at the feathery contact. Finally her voice, soft as rose petals.

"Chase."

His name. Just his name. And imbued in it was every emotion, every need, every desire.

He took her by the hand and led her to the bedroom. With deliberate care he folded back the linens, unwrapped the bath towel from her and guided her onto the open expanse of sheet, bending over her and kissing her flat against the mattress.

"Just think about me, about us, about this," he said against her lips. "I'll be back."

Tessa watched him leave the room. When she heard the shower come on, she stretched and smiled, much like a lazy cat luxuriating in a sunbeam, although the twilight cast more shadow than illumination. Still, she was warm from the shower, warmer from her imagination, bordering on hot from anticipation. She basked in the sensuality of what they'd shared and drew measured breaths of wonder, of desire, of expectation—and just a little impatience.

He returned, and she admired the artistry of his body, a masterpiece of muscle and flesh. His arousal flattered her, bewitched her, pleased her. He knelt beside her, saying nothing, and she used the tip of her finger to swirl the drop that spilled from him like a promise. His breathing deepened. She indulged her fantasies then, as he slid his fingers into her hair and clamped her head. And it was wondrous and exciting and soul shattering to show him her love in such a powerful and intimate way.

His body shook. He pulled her up to devour her mouth, kissing her with a staggering desperation, his hands imprisoned in her hair, his throat vibrating with deep sounds of need. Finally he laid her down and draped her legs over his thighs. She closed her eyes and drifted....

Enjoying his power way too much, Chase dragged a pillow under her hips. He teased her, explored her, cherished the differences of their genders. She became a wild thing, all moans and quivers and thrusts, primal and unforgettable in her need, beautiful in her openness. He bent over, loving her with his mouth as she exploded once. Twice. Once more. Pulling her up, he impaled her on himself and she locked him inside her and took him higher than he'd ever been.

"I love you," she cried. "I love you."

And he knew the moment would live forever in his dreams; delight and torment both. He wouldn't forget her all-woman body or her pure-woman fragrance or her perfect-woman taste. He wouldn't forget the eager gentleness of her touch. He would hear her words of love echo in his mind until the day he died—and hear the tenderness and the surety and the desperation.

But he knew he couldn't say the words to her in return. Not now. Not ever. It was the most dishonest thing he'd done in his life, not to tell her he loved her, too.

She went still against him, her face buried against his shoulder, her arms wrapped around him, clinging as if the world were about to end. The sharp, rich scent of lovemaking reached his nose and he memorized it.

"Chase," she said quietly, so quietly he almost didn't hear.

He combed her hair with his fingers, offering comfort to the tension he could hear beneath the hushed tone. "What?"

"We didn't use birth control." She leaned back. Her face drained of color. "Last week it didn't matter. This week...I don't know."

He didn't have a clue what to say to her. He'd drummed responsibility and consequences into the kids' heads for years. Where had his own common sense flown?

"Say something."

"What can I say, Tessa? We'll cross that bridge if we come to it."

"Destiny," she whispered.

"Accountability."

Tessa moved out of the circle of his arms as she felt his resignation snake through her, cold and slithery. This was no fantasy to him, as it was to her. No matter how much she believed in the inevitability of what had happened between them, he was much too practical to agree.

She didn't want to lose what had been so special about the day. The funny moment when he'd admitted to liking the romance novel. The difficult revelations of her past. The playfulness in the ocean. The lovemaking that got freer and better every time.

"What are you thinking?" he asked, resting against the headboard and reaching for her hand.

She pressed his hand to her cheek, then kissed his palm. "That I'm glad you haven't been intimate with another woman. That you haven't made memories with anyone else. I guess that's selfish, but it makes me very happy."

"That's not selfishness. It's human nature."

"I didn't know why I was waiting all those years. I just knew I hadn't found it yet," she said, snuggling against him, her ear pressed to his chest, her arm around him. His arms encircled her, a safe haven she never wanted to leave. "I had opportunities with other men. Nothing ever felt right. But the day I walked into your office, I knew you'd be the one."

He drew tiny circles on her skin with his fingers. "Do you remember when I left you alone that day while you were filling out the paperwork?"

She nodded, loving the way his skin felt against hers.

"I was fantasizing about you. I had to get away for a minute."

She tipped her head back to look at him. "You must have had opportunities with other women."

"I avoided most opportunities."

"Most?" She watched his lips twitch slightly. "Never mind. I don't want details." She cuddled against him again, closed her eyes and cherished the quiet, tender moment. After a minute she felt his hand settle on her abdomen, creating a shield, protective and insulating. The gesture comforted and lulled her—and gave her hope.

"Would it bother you so much?" she asked. It was a huge question, phrased simply, but with entire futures awaiting the answer.

"What?"

She blanketed his hand with hers. "If we made a baby."

"Yes."

When she tried to pull away, he tightened his hold on her.

"I know that's not the answer you want to hear, Tessa, but it's the truth. And that's not to say I wouldn't do the right thing. But we deserve to have choices. I hope that in acting irresponsibly, I didn't take those choices away."

"It wouldn't be your fault alone."

"I'm sorry. That's all I can say."

She sighed and closed her eyes. "Me, too."

Early the next morning, Chase moved quietly out of the bathroom and into his bedroom. He glanced at the clock on the nightstand, deciding he might as well head out now, before Tessa woke up. Before she could try to talk him out of going. He'd spent most of the night awake, holding her, soothing her when she stirred, seeming to sense what the next day would bring.

*Could you kill for her?*

The question loomed, larger than ever. He wouldn't know the answer until he was forced to decide.

Indulging himself, Chase crouched beside the bed to watch her sleep for a minute longer. An image of her pregnant, her body lush and rounded, moseyed through his imagination. He didn't allow the picture to burn into his memory.

Standing, he moved silently across the room, slid open a dresser drawer and withdrew an envelope. Folding it in half, he jammed it in his jacket pocket.

"Good morning."

He turned around at the sound of her voice. Propped on her

elbows, she smiled at him, her eyes sleepy, her shoulders naked above the quilt that otherwise covered her modestly.

"Going somewhere?" she asked, her gaze sweeping down him. "We've got plenty of stuff for breakfast."

He sat beside her on the bed. She snuggled into the pillow as he brushed her wild hair away from her face. The well that had filled inside him over the past few weeks began to drain, a slow emptying of the happiness he never expected to have—and didn't deserve—but which had poured into him anyway, unbidden, tormenting him with hope and need.

"This is Sunday," she said, her voice filled with sudden realization, the morning warmth disappearing from her in an instant. "The first Sunday of the month." She sat up. The quilt fell away as she clutched his jacket. "The envelope you took from the drawer— It's for Brent, isn't it? There's money in it."

"Yes."

"Oh, please, Chase. Don't go. Don't do this."

"I have to."

"You've paid your debt. Make him get on with his life."

"I know you don't understand."

"I understand plenty." Tessa couldn't argue with him when she was naked. Needing some kind of armor, she climbed out of bed and went in search of her robe, which she'd left on the hook inside the bathroom door. "Don't go anywhere," she said as she left the room, feeling his gaze on her.

She found him a couple minutes later in the living room, staring out the window. She'd taken the time to splash water on her face, brush her teeth, weave her hair into a loose braid—and calm her nerves. She'd never known a more principled man, which was an admirable and exasperating fact about him, and one of the reasons she loved him.

She came up beside him. "There's nothing I can say to change your mind, is there? No matter how much I beg? No matter how many times I tell you that you're hurting Brent—and yourself— by continuing this."

He didn't look at her. "Nothing."

She wondered what he saw when he looked out the window—or if he saw anything at all. Hurt warred with anger within her. She wanted him to listen to her. She also knew when she was defeated. "When will you be back?"

Seconds ticked by. Seconds filled by the worst silence she'd ever known.

"You're scaring me," she said, barely able to get the words out.

"I called Les this morning. She's coming over in about an hour to take you to Gabe's house. You're going to stay there until this is over."

She felt as if he'd slapped her. "Am I?" Her cold, flat voice belied the fury building within her.

"He's got plenty of room, and you'll be safe there."

"This is for my own good, I suppose." Colder, flatter, more furious. "How dare you decide what's best for me? How dare you?"

He turned to her then, and she saw something flash across his face, something she hoped she wasn't reading correctly—because he looked as if this were the last time he would see her. Fear and dread replaced her anger over his unasked-for management of her life.

"I can't keep you here any longer, Tessa. This is killing me. And it's slow and painful, and more agony than I can bear. You know we can't have a future."

"I'm sorry I lied to you, Chase. But we can get past that. We can."

*"Don't you get it?"*

She hadn't heard him shout before. The volume startled her. His fierce expression made her take a step back.

"This isn't about lying. This is about family. Do you suppose your family could look at me, year in and year out, and not be reminded of what happened? Could they? You know them. Could they forgive me? I know that *you* have, but from everything you've said, they couldn't. I can't ask you to choose between us. That would be even worse. We couldn't be together and be happy. You'd be miserable without your family. And there isn't any way I could make that up to you.''

"If it came to a choice, I'd choose you." She reached out to him but he moved away. "We are destined—"

"There's no such thing as destiny! There's only what's right. And this isn't right. You take your family for granted, Tessa. You need to stop and consider your life without them. I know—I *know*—how precious family is. And I'm not taking you from yours.''

He folded his arms over his chest. His voice gentled. "Tessa. I didn't have a family. No father. No siblings. A mother who never parented me. Sarge was the closest thing I had to a parent, but he wanted me to toe the line. He didn't—and doesn't—show affection, although I know he cares for me. But you grew up in a house where you knew you were loved. You don't know what you'd be asking of yourself if you had to give that up."

"It's because of that love that I must believe they wouldn't disown me if I choose you." She took a step closer to him. "What if I'm pregnant?''

His face went blank. He must have forgotten the possibility.

"I won't have an abortion, Chase.''

He turned his back on her.

She flattened her hands against his shoulder blades, then slid her arms around him, resting her cheek against his back. "Family,'' she said softly. "Your own family.''

"God, Tessa! Why are you doing this to me? Why do you continue to torture me with something I can't have?''

"Because you don't owe anyone anything. Not anymore. Because you're the most deserving person I know—even if you refuse to believe that about yourself.''

"Maybe in time I could. But it can't be you. Don't you see that? *It can't be you.*''

"You'd choose someone else?''

Chase felt her arms tighten around him, could feel her body tense against his. He might lie by omission, but he wouldn't directly lie to her. No, he wouldn't choose someone else. Couldn't. She wasn't thinking clearly. She wasn't looking far enough into the future.

*What if I'm pregnant?*

That would change everything—except for what he had to do today.

"I have to go," he said, pushing her arms down. "Please don't take your anger out on Les. Or Gabe. They're only doing what I'm asking."

He walked to the front door. He wouldn't turn around. His memories would suffice. The best ones.

But he glanced back when he grabbed the knob and saw her looking so sad, so disillusioned. So lost.

"Don't cry, Tessa. Please don't cry."

She ran into his arms and he kissed her as tears flowed down her cheeks, so that all he tasted was heat and salt and goodbye mixed together. It wasn't the way he wanted to remember her. He wanted to remember her softness and her smile. Her tender heart. The strong woman and the hesitant virgin.

How could one person have so many dimensions? He walked down an unswerving path. She danced through cloverleaf turns, explored exits, then found her way back onto the straight road again for a while. He envied her that. He wished he'd been allowed to take her hand and go wherever she led, exploring the world together.

But he couldn't. The price was too high. For now he'd content himself with the knowledge she was safe. Les and Gabe would see to that.

And Chase would put an end to the threat now.

*Could you kill for her?*

There was only one way to find out.

# Thirteen

Tessa folded the last of her clothes and stuffed them into her suitcase, muttering to herself all the while. Chase had been gone for almost half an hour, but she refused to believe that by walking out the door, he was walking out of her life. She could do something for him, however. She could leave, just as he asked. Not because she was in the mood to be obedient—he was wrong about everything, after all—but because if absence made the heart grow fonder, she was willing to try it.

Not, however, by moving into Gabe's house.

Absolutely not. If she wanted to put someone else in jeopardy along with herself, she'd go to her parents' house and lay the groundwork for getting them to accept Chase, to grant him the forgiveness he needed and to give her and Chase their blessing. But that would have to stay a dream for a while. She couldn't put her family in danger by going to them. She'd already had to lie to them about going out of town for a seminar, while instead she had stayed with Chase.

Nor would she involve a virtual stranger, no matter how long he'd been Chase's friend.

The danger was real, though, and to ignore it would be downright stupid, if not suicidal. Somehow she had to make it back to her apartment without being seen, exchange dirty clothes for clean ones, then check into a hotel.

If she kept busy enough, she could avoid thinking about everything that had happened with Chase earlier. She couldn't stop. Couldn't slow down. Couldn't give her thoughts a chance to drift, or else she'd remember the look on his face and the desperation in his kiss and the determination in his voice.

She carried her suitcase into the living room and set it by the front door, then made a final walk-through of his apartment. She'd intentionally left a few items—her hand lotion, a nightgown, the T-shirt he said matched her eyes perfectly. In return, she took a T-shirt of his, with the intention of wearing it to bed every night until he was beside her again.

Obsession. It had only been a word before. Now it defined her life. She was beginning to understand the man obsessed with her, and that scared her.

Tessa made her way down the stairs and through the Center, which wouldn't open for another hour. She waited at the front door until she heard a car horn, then she left the safety of the Center to climb into a taxicab. She asked the driver to take her by the park where she knew Chase met Brent, and she saw them in deep discussion—and saw Chase pass her brother the envelope. Hope burst from her like a popped balloon. Devoid of emotion, she gave the driver her address, then changed her mind and told him to take her back to where they started.

A willing human target, Chase wandered through the neighborhood, eager for a confrontation. He didn't own a weapon, but his hands were strong and his mind clear. He'd left Tessa at the Center not only physically but emotionally, blocking her almost completely from his thoughts. Visions of her brother lingered, however. Giving Brent the money had become automatic through the years—until this time.

He didn't want to think about that now. He needed to focus only on today, to be aware of everyone and everything around him. Then he could deal with his losses.

He walked the streets until faces blurred into vague images and voices blended into a cacophony of sound without meaning. He knew he should take a break and let his head clear again, but where should he go? He needed to check in with Les or Gabe, both of whom complained constantly because he refused to get a cellular phone or a beeper.

He was only a few blocks from the Center. If he didn't go up to his apartment, he could handle being there, with its familiar sights and sounds. He'd make a couple of calls, rest his eyes for a few minutes, then return to his reconnaissance. He wanted this over with. Today.

A car horn blared. Gabe. *Gabe?*

"Get in!" Gabe shouted. He touched a button on the visor and Chase heard a familiar voice come over a speaker.

"O'Keefe."

"I've got him, Les. We'll be there in three minutes." Gabe disconnected the call. "Where the hell have you been?"

"What's going on?" Chase asked, dreading the answer. "Why aren't you home with Tessa?"

"Because Tessa has disappeared."

*"What?"* Fear strangled any other words.

"Les went to pick her up, and found only her suitcase, which was just inside the front door. But no note explaining anything. No clues as to where she went. The door was locked. There weren't signs of forced entry. Les called Sarge, who had opted not to tell anyone that you had plans to turn vigilante. Thanks for clueing me in, pal. Thanks a lot."

"Not a vigilante. I just wanted to draw him out. Anyway, it was my problem—"

"Like hell. Eighteen years of friendship means nothing to you? You should have told me. First Sebastian, and now you."

Chase needed to stay calm. Needed a clear head. Gabe's injured feelings were the least of his worries. "How long ago did Les discover Tessa was gone?"

"An hour, maybe a little longer. Les was late picking her up. At first she thought maybe Tessa had gone home on her own, but she didn't pick up the phone at her apartment. Les sent a patrol car out. No one answered the door. Then she remembered she had Tessa's house key, anyway, because she picked up the mail yesterday, I gather. So Tessa probably couldn't have gone there if she'd wanted to."

"Where is Les now?"

"At the Center with Sarge. I was just headed there."

Although Chase scanned the street in search of any sign of Tessa, he felt his friend's gaze leveled on him.

"We'll find her."

Chase nodded, believing it, not accepting any other possibility. She was smart and clever and well trained—and already on alert. *So, why hasn't anyone heard from her?*

Gabe double-parked behind a police car. They flung open the doors, then took the stairs three at a time, synchronized, determined. Chase's pulse thundered. He focused on his heartbeat, rhythmic and life affirming, as he tamped down the panic that threatened. It didn't matter who else helped in the search. No one had as much at stake as he did—therefore he needed the most control, the most logical mind, the surest plan.

*What if I'm pregnant?*

The remembered question, asked with such hope, emblazoned itself on his mind as he punched open the door to the Center and jogged into the unnaturally quiet building. Fear shone in the eyes of every child he saw as he ran to his office, or perhaps they were just mirroring him. He nodded reassurance, wishing he could offer comfort, needing comfort himself.

When Chase rushed into his office he saw Leslie seated at his desk, talking on the phone, and Sarge stationed by the window, scanning the street.

"Fill me in," Chase demanded.

Leslie held up a finger. "Yeah. Call my cell phone, in case I've left." She cradled the receiver. "Chase." She stood. "After this is over, we're having a talk about—"

"Stuff it, Les. What's going on with Tessa?"

"I don't have any news. Gabe told you what happened?"

"Yeah." He ran his hands through his hair, locked his fingers behind his neck. "No one's seen or heard from her? Her parents? Neighbors?"

"No one. I've got patrol cars cruising everywhere. If she's around, we'll see her."

*If she's around*... "Did you check my apartment? I know it seems obvious, but there is another entrance, and—"

"She's not there."

Chase joined Sarge at the window.

"We don't even know if foul play is involved, Chase. Nothing indicates that."

"The attack doesn't count? The letter can be ignored, Les? There's foul play here. I know it. I feel it." He stopped, hearing his own words. He didn't believe in destiny. Or fate. Or psychic links. And yet...he knew she was in trouble. "I know I sound crazy."

"No," Leslie said. "You sound like a man in love."

Silence settled in the room for a few seconds.

"We have to find her, Les," Chase said with a calmness he didn't feel. "Now. Something's wrong."

"Mr. Ryan?"

Everyone turned at once at the intrusion.

"Bobby. This isn't a good time," Leslie said.

The teenager came into the room, not making eye contact, his in-your-face attitude gone. He shifted his weight. "I heard...I heard you talkin' 'bout Miss Rose." He swallowed. "Maybe I can help, you know?"

"How?" Chase asked, trying not to get his hopes up.

Bobby looked at everyone's faces finally, then focused on Chase. "I was hangin' for a while out front, waitin' for the place to open. Thought maybe I'd take a look. See if I liked it here."

Trying not to rush the boy, Chase nodded.

"Anyway, Miss Rose, she got into a taxi. Had a suitcase with her, and she looked—I don't know. Mad? Something. She's gone ten, maybe fifteen minutes, then the cab pulls up again and she gets out. She hurries up the stairs, unlocks the door, then she shoves her suitcase in and gets back in the cab. They take off. This time she's not mad. She looked kinda— You know how people who get bad news look? Like that. Old, kinda."

Leslie flipped open her phone. "Do you know which cab company?"

"The one with the yellow cars. But there's somethin' else." He shoved his hands in his pockets. "Somebody else was hangin' out, too. Some guy. Waitin' across the street. Waitin' and watchin'. When Miss Rose came out the first time, he paid real close attention, you know? You could tell he was tryin' to hear what she was sayin' to the cabdriver. He ran up the street a few blocks followin' the car, but pretty soon he couldn't keep up."

"What did he look like?" Chase asked, deadly calm.

Bobby looked at the floor. "Kinda the same build as the guy who got her the other day."

"Kind of?"

"Not as big as you, Mr. Ryan."

"Did you see his face?"

"Nah. He was wearin' a hat."

Chase felt his blood dam up in every artery. "What color?"

"Blue."

Leslie picked up her cell phone and dialed 411, then passed a piece of paper Sarge's way. "Dodger's address. Call it in. I'll get the cab company."

"It's bad, huh?" Bobby swore. "I knew it. I'm sorry, Mr. Ryan. I like Miss Rose. I shoulda done something."

Absently Chase patted the boy's shoulder. "You did."

"Sooner. I'm stupid, just like my dad says. Stupid. Never amount to nothin'."

Chase turned toward Gabe, imploring him silently, grateful when Gabe took the boy aside to reassure him.

Dodger. He'd been right all along. Why hadn't he forced the issue before? Like Bobby, he'd ignored his instincts, and now Tessa was paying the price.

"Fisherman's Wharf," Leslie said to the room at large, then tipped the receiver toward her mouth again. "I want to talk to the driver. Get a hold of him and have him call this number immediately."

Fisherman's Wharf? What kind of sense did that make? Why would Tessa go to one of the biggest tourist attractions in San Francisco, one she'd probably been to a hundred times? And why had she come back to the Center and left her suitcase? Why had she come back at all? And where had she been headed the first time?

Why hadn't she done what he'd asked of her, then she'd be safe with Gabe right now instead of—

He didn't want to think about the "instead of," and asking himself questions accomplished nothing. He couldn't stand here feeling helpless for one more second. He had to do something.

"You don't suppose she's just spending the afternoon playing tourist, do you?" Leslie asked, clearly puzzled. "Is that something she would do?"

*"How the hell am I supposed to know?"*

He hadn't uttered a profane word in his life, not even in his mind. He swiped a hand across his mouth.

Leslie's cell phone chirped. She questioned the cabdriver for several minutes, then ended the call. "He said he picked her up, drove a few blocks at her specific direction, but she changed her mind and asked to be brought back here. She left the suitcase, then told him to take her to the Wharf. That was that, apparently.

He said she seemed very sad and didn't want to talk." She stood. "Sarge? What've you got?"

"Unit's on the way to Dodger's residence."

"Okay. I want to be there, too. Chase, I know it won't do any good to tell you to stay here, so you might as well come with me."

Tessa rummaged through her purse twice before she remembered she'd given her house key to Leslie yesterday. Great. This was just great. She was tired and hungry and sweaty from spending hours at the Wharf wandering with the tourists, losing herself in the crowds and noise, and now she couldn't even get into her apartment.

And if she called Leslie and asked her to bring the key, Leslie would insist on taking her to Gabe's house—the plan according to Chase Ryan. Since Tessa still had no intention of following The Plan, she had to decide what to do. Without fresh clothes, without a shower.

There was no on-site landlord who would have a key, and she hadn't given a duplicate to anyone. She couldn't go to a hotel without a change of clothes.

Realizing she didn't have much choice, she decided to call Leslie. Tessa would deal with the repercussions of making the call when Leslie arrived, woman to woman, not just Chase's-friend to Chase's-rejected-lover. Leslie seemed like a straightforward, no-nonsense kind of woman. She would understand Tessa's need to stay independent, and her need not to risk someone else's life.

Having rationalized her situation, Tessa knocked on Norm's door to ask if she could use his phone, wanting to avoid being out on the street, if she could help it. She wished she knew her other neighbors. Norm's girlfriend—what was her name? Marcy? She lived downstairs, but Tessa couldn't remember her apartment number.

When no one answered, she started toward the stairs intent on finding a pay phone.

"Tess! Hi!" Norm called out from below. "Long time, no see." He jogged up the stairs. "How are you?"

"I'm fine, thanks. How are you?"

"Great. Been staying with your boyfriend?"

"Yes."

"Any more trouble from that guy who attacked you?" He walked past her and unlocked his door.

"No. Listen, could I ask a favor of you? Could I use your phone to make a call? I'm locked out of my apartment."

"Sure." He swept his baseball cap off his head and smiled. "Just ignore the mess. Today is cleaning day but I haven't started yet."

"I won't stay long. I have to call someone's pager, then wait for a return call. Are you sure I'm not putting you out?"

"Not at all. We have to shut the door fast, though, or else my cats will sneak out."

"I didn't know you had cats."

"It's not public knowledge. There's a no-pets rule here, you know."

Tessa did know. She was such a rule follower herself that she wouldn't dream of breaking established regulations, even though she'd wanted a kitten along with a place of her own. "How's Marcy?" she asked as she slipped through the doorway—then stopped abruptly and caught her breath. The stench was incredible, and seemed to be coming from two litter boxes that hadn't been cleaned in a long time.

At least four cats lifted their heads from a sofa and chairs to look at the human intruders. Tessa's skin crawled. She didn't want to breathe, didn't want to stay another second in the apartment that smelled like—

Her stomach clenched as a terrifyingly graphic image lit up her mind.

The apartment smelled like the ski mask.

Norm was right behind her, so close she could hear him breathe.

"Marcy and I broke up," he said.

*Stay calm. Figure out your next step. Don't let him get an advantage.*

The words replayed in her mind as she looked around for an escape route. If she could move a few steps, she'd have room to swing around and catch him by surprise. At the moment he could pin her against the wall.

Open space. She needed open space. She turned around, affixed a smile on her face.

"Where's the phone?"

"Oh, buried under something." He lifted a hand, turned the key in the dead bolt, then dropped it into his pants' pocket. "What's your hurry?"

Locked in. Fear as unyielding as barbed wire held her in place. "Unlock the door, Norm."

"I don't think so, babe. And this time I'm ready for whatever fancy moves you want to make."

A psychopathic smile curved his mouth. "Don't act so surprised. I can tell you know it was me who went after you."

"Why did you? What had I done to you?" She took half a step back. Being locked in changed everything. She had to knock him unconscious to get the key. This time she searched the room for something to use.

"I promised your father."

"What?"

He took a step toward her. "The day you moved in. I helped your dad bring your couch up the stairs, remember?"

She took an equivalent step back. "I remember."

"He was worried about you being alone. I told him I'd look out for you. We shook hands on it, you know. You were supposed to be a good girl, Tess. He said you were. But you were necking on the stairs just a couple of days after you moved in. Your father wouldn't have been pleased. You were my responsibility."

He reached for her, and she spun out of arm's length. "Why the attack? What did you expect to accomplish?" If she just kept him talking, she might get him to relax, then she could strike.

"I figured you'd stay at home then, like you were supposed to. Instead, you turn to that man who made you not a good girl anymore. He's got you under some kinda spell, Tess. But don't worry. I'll help you forget him. I can make you clean again. Then your father will be happy."

A hero complex? That's what this was about? He thought he was protecting her? "I don't need any help, Norm. I'm in love with that man. He's wonderful, and I'm committed to him."

"Is that why you took your suitcase when you left his place this morning?"

*He'd seen her? He'd been staking her out?* Nausea threatened. She couldn't even draw deep breaths to counteract it, the litter box odor was so overwhelming, the remembered smell bringing back vivid memories. He may have just been trying to scare her, but the violence she'd battled was too real.

"I was coming home to pick up more clothes." She moved back another few inches. Her stomach roiled.

He reached around her, slid open a drawer and pulled out the sweater she'd been wearing that day. He rubbed it across his face. "Your father doesn't know you're sleeping around. It's not too late. He likes me. And now that I know you're not daddy's little girl, there's only one thing to do with you."

He grinned, undoubtedly taking pleasure in her revulsion.

"What's the matter, babe? You've been around the block a time or two, that's easy to see. Sex was created with you in mind. But you're wasted on *him.* Anyone could see he wasn't right for you." He moved closer, filling the space she'd eked out between them. "You'll forget all about him once you've been with me."

"Sex happens between consenting adults," she said, backing up. Her hand touched a paperweight. Was it heavy enough to knock him out? "It's a decision for both people involved, not just the man."

"So you're a tease, too. That's okay. I like that part of the game. When a woman says no, I know she means yes. I know she just wants to be convinced."

"Women say no when they mean no. I repeat—I'm in a committed relationship. I'm not going to sleep with you."

"Who's talking about sleep, babe? I knew you wanted me that first day when I helped you move in. The way you flaunted your body at me. I was surprised when I saw you with...*him*."

Outside the door, across the hall, someone knocked.

"Tessa!" More knocking.

She closed her fingers around the paperweight. "Chase! In here, I'm—"

Norm shoved her aside. The paperweight slipped to the floor. He raced to a desk and yanked open the top drawer as the front door cracked with the force of Chase's weight.

"He's got a knife!" she yelled.

Wood splintered, flying everywhere. Chase burst through the shattered door. Tessa kicked Norm's hand. The knife flew across the room, hit a wall, then dropped with a clatter of metal against wood.

Chase slammed into him, driving him against a bookcase, the force sending knickknacks everywhere. He drove his fist into Norm's stomach, once. Again. Norm connected with his fist to Chase's jaw.

An unstoppable force now, Chase pummeled Norm until he doubled over—then kept on hitting.

"Chase, stop!" she grabbed his arm. "You'll kill him!"

Someone climbed through the hole in the door. Bobby Moran.

"Help me," Tessa begged. "We have to stop him."

Bobby insinuated himself between the men, calling Chase's name, pushing him back as Tessa pulled. Norm crumpled to the floor. Legs apart and locked, Chase gulped in air, his fists clenched, his eyes on the man, daring him to stand up again.

"Don't do it, man," Bobby said, panting as well.

Chase shifted his glance to Bobby, coming aware of where he

was and what had happened. He turned his head. Tessa stood there, her eyes wide, her face ashen, her arms folded across her stomach.

"Are you all right?" he demanded.

She nodded. Her eyes filled, then she took a step toward him. One more. Two. She flung herself into his arms.

"Oh, thank God you got here in time. Thank God."

"Shh. Shh." He stroked her hair, tried not to hold her too close or too dearly. He'd already said his goodbyes to her.

Footsteps pounded the stairs, then a group of people appeared and came into the room, one by one, with Leslie leading the way. Then Sarge. A couple of uniformed officers. Gabe.

"Good instincts," Leslie said to Chase as the officers hauled Norm to his feet and handcuffed him.

Chase released Tessa. She tried to take his hand but he moved away from her. He would like to chalk it up to instincts, but it was much more than instinct that had led him here when everyone else had gone in search of Dodger. He hadn't suspected Norm. He just had a feeling…

But he refused to call it destiny.

"What do you mean, good instincts?" Tessa asked Leslie.

"We'd concluded that we were looking for Dodger. Most of us went in search of him. Not Chase. Of course he told me he'd stay by the phone, which he didn't. But I guess it worked out."

"Thanks to Bobby, too," Chase said, putting a hand on the young man's shoulder. "I would've killed the scum." He looked at Sarge then. *Does that answer your question?*

Sarge nodded, as silent as Chase.

"What brought you here, Les?" Chase asked.

"First, Dodger had an alibi. He'd been with someone all day, so he couldn't have been hanging out by the Center. I'd ordered that I be notified on any activity in the neighborhood. While we were at Dodger's, I got word that Norm's ex-girlfriend filed a sexual battery complaint against him this morning."

Conversation stopped as Norm was led away.

"What about the cats?"

Everyone left turned toward Tessa, who was crouching and holding out her hand, trying to pet one of the cats.

"Look at them, poor things. They're so scared."

"I'll call animal control," Leslie said. "Then I need a statement from you. Chase and Bobby, too. At the station would be best. Bobby, maybe you should give your dad a call and have him meet us."

"Okay."

Leslie bent over and picked up something from the floor.

"The sweater he took from me last week," Tessa said.

Leslie pulled a large baggie from her pocket and dropped it in, then she crouched beside Tessa. "How are you?"

"I'm okay."

Chase didn't want to hear their conversation. He walked over to Sarge and Gabe.

"Why aren't you comforting her?" Gabe asked. "She's in shock."

Chase folded his arms across his chest. "Remember the boy who was shot and paralyzed in the store? That was Tessa's brother."

Gabe swore.

"Do you think there's a future for us, given our pasts?" Chase asked.

"I don't know. I've never seen you so happy, so I'm probably prejudiced. But it seems to me that it's her decision. If she can live with it, you can."

His gaze settled on Tessa as she cradled one of the cats. She stroked its fur, soothing it, and he could feel her touch himself. Happy? Yes, he'd been happy. But that was then.

He looked straight at Gabe. "I can't," he said, then he walked away.

# Fourteen

**H**ours passed before they were through with questioning. By some unspoken agreement, no one offered to drive Tessa home, leaving Chase to do it. When they reached her apartment, they looked at the boarded-up door across from hers, then ignored it. She felt his complete withdrawal from her in the absence of touch, of conversation, of tender gazes. She unlocked her door, opened it, then stood waiting for him to say something. He didn't.

"Do you want my resignation from the Center?" she asked.

He hesitated. "That would be best."

"For whom?" she muttered. "Not me. Frankly, I'm tired of you getting your way on everything."

"I told your brother this was the last time I would give him money."

The surprising statement caught her off guard.

"I gave it a lot of thought," he said. "We both needed it to stop."

She nodded, her throat closing. "Thank you."

"I'm a different man from the one you met a few weeks ago, Tessa. I'd held on to my guilt as tightly as my virginity. When I gave up one, the other followed. I have you to thank for that."

"But you haven't changed enough to share the rest of your life with me."

"I can't let you turn your back on your family."

"Do you love me?" She laid a hand against his chest. "I need to know that much. Please."

Long seconds passed. Long, heartbreaking seconds. "Yes."

"Say the words."

"I can't. I can only answer your question."

"You're a warm, giving man. You deserve a family. A real family. If you don't believe I can give you that, then I want you to find someone who can. And if you don't think that's the biggest sacrifice I've ever made, then you don't know me at all. I love you with all my heart. I always will. You *are* my destiny."

She took his hand and pressed it to her abdomen. "But I don't want you by default. So, it's now or never. Maybe I'm pregnant. Maybe not. If I am, I won't tell you. I'll go away where you'll never find me, because I won't be something you *had* to do. Someone you had to marry. Can you live with that?"

"That's blackmail."

"Call it what you will. I'm fighting for my life here."

"How can I live with myself if I take you from your family?" he asked, harsh and low.

"How can you live with yourself if we made a baby and you're not part of his life? We love each other. It'll be enough. I promise you that."

"I don't believe you wouldn't tell me."

He knew her too well. But she couldn't back down now. She'd started the debate, planted the doubt in his head. She had to see it through. "Like you, I'll do what I have to do."

Chase studied her. He hadn't realized how well matched they were. He'd always focused on their differences, not their similarities. "Will you give me until tomorrow?" he asked, needing time to think, time to sort.

"If I have to."

"All right. Tomorrow."

"Should I come to work?"

He'd forgotten. Tomorrow was Monday. "Yes, then come to my office at eight o'clock, when you're done."

"All right."

Tessa watched him go, wishing she could conjure up some clever farewell line, but fresh out of witticisms. The entire conversation had been civilized—too civilized. She admired him more than anyone she knew. He would devote himself to a marriage and family the way he had to his work, and she wanted more than anything to be the subject of his devotion. But she meant what she'd said—she didn't want him by default.

She shut her apartment door and looked around the room, which seemed so empty now. The independence she'd fought for had amounted to a total of about two weeks on her own. It had been long enough. Amazing what the right person could do to change someone's goals. She'd just never expected that loving someone could be so hard.

Her calendar beckoned her. She counted off days and decided there was little chance of her being pregnant, so that threat wouldn't amount to anything. Which was good. She thought.

Well, she had about twenty-four hours to wait. To worry. To dream. Tomorrow at this time it would be over. Questions answered. Futures determined.

Just like her first day in her new apartment, she stripped right there in the middle of the living room, this time heading for the shower. First she would wash away the day, send it right down the drain. Norm was crazy. He probably wouldn't end up in jail, but in some psychiatric facility. Tessa didn't care, as long as he was gone.

Memories assaulted her as she stood under the steamy warmth of her shower. The reel in her head ran backward. The feel of

Chase's hand against her abdomen. The fury on his face as he burst through Norm's door. The exquisite pleasure of his lovemaking.

His smile. His laugh, heard only once but cherished.

Too few kisses, too many heart-wrenching goodbyes.

Sharing homemade cookies, sharing pain, sharing dreams.

The boy. Tessa focused on the image of long ago, with a new perspective now. She'd been sympathetic to him then. Knowing his past only endeared him to her more. Maybe she was being fanciful. Maybe her sense of destiny was distorted by other things, like physical pleasure. She didn't think so, but how could she tell for sure?

Did anyone really fall in love that fast?

Insecurity settled over her. She turned off the shower water, then sat cross-legged in the tub, her hair a wet blanket down her back. She wouldn't have made love with him without being *in* love with him, right? She'd waited all these years because she was waiting for the right man, the man she would love until she died. Right?

Of course, she had been attracted to him from the beginning. A heart-pounding, libido teasing, let's-see-how-fast-we-can-get-undressed-and-in-bed attraction. She closed her eyes, remembering. She loved the way he looked, the way he smelled, the way his body felt. She loved the strength and power of him—everywhere. He'd taken her to paradise so many times she'd stopped counting. Enough times to lose most of her shyness. She'd loved making love with him.

She blinked her eyes open. But did she *love* him? Did she love *him?* Was she confusing love and sex and desire and whatever else was going on here?

The thought scared her. Was it all a fantasy? Had she turned his life upside down along with hers...unnecessarily?

She wished he was here. She didn't want to face the whole night confused, worried, *wrong.* If she was wrong, how could she tell him now? Maybe a small part of her had wanted to rebel against her family, who'd tied her so relentlessly to them all these years.

Was Chase her rebellion?

Panicked now that she was making the biggest mistake of her life, Tessa dried off and dressed in sweatpants and a T-shirt. She paced her apartment, flopped onto the sofa, shoved herself up again, then paced some more.

Now that the idea had taken root, she was sure she was wrong. She didn't know what love was! How could she? A few weeks wasn't long enough to make that kind of determination.

What had she done?

She scooped up a windbreaker, tied on her sneakers, grabbed her keys and left the apartment. She wouldn't make him spend the evening alone in his apartment debating, worrying, trying to make a lifetime decision because she'd forced him into it. No way. She was a fair person.

She would put him out of his misery.

She heard laughter and grunts and a ball bouncing and deep male voices. Tessa slid the key to the Center's front door into her pocket and headed toward the sounds, toward the gymnasium. Cautious, she peeked inside. Gabe and Ben were playing basketball—with Chase.

Well! So much for his being alone and miserable.

"Chase Ryan!"

Instant silence, punctuated by the fading sound of a loose basketball, followed her shout into the cavernous gym. She marched in, hands curled into fists, her face heating up. It was infuriating the way he was having fun while she'd been struggling with her feelings. Had been tormented! At the very least he should be in his apartment by himself, but here he was with his friends enjoying—enjoying—a game of basketball. They all watched her approach.

"Careful," Gabe said to Chase. "She's strutting. You know what that means."

"She's mad."

"More like outraged. And feeling righteous about something," Ben answered, toeing the ball up from the floor and into his hands, then holding it against one hip. "What'd you do?"

"I didn't do anything. Not that I know of."

"Wrong. You did something. That's moral indignation, if ever I've seen it," Gabe said, a thoughtful tone in his voice. "Didn't even take the time to put on a bra. You ticked her off good."

Tessa tugged her jacket across her chest, but didn't slow down. She heard every word they said. His friends might be teasing him, but he was genuinely bewildered. Wasn't that just like a man?

"Give me the ball," she said to Ben, although her gaze never left Chase.

Ben chuckled, earning himself a missile of a glare. He swallowed, then he bounced the ball to her.

"One-on-one," she said to Chase.

"Why?"

"I think she's got more than basketball in mind," Gabe said with a grin.

Tessa scowled at him.

He laughed. "Ben. How about dinner? My treat?"

"Excellent idea, Gabriel. Thanks."

They swept up jackets and wallets and keys and headed out the door, elbowing each other. Tessa barely noticed.

"What's got you so fired up?" Chase asked when they were alone.

"You're having fun!"

He waited a few beats. "So?"

"So you're supposed to be...to be...miserable. Like me."

"You're going to have to explain that."

She wedged the ball between her knees, stripped off her jacket and tossed it aside. She bounced the ball, then she made a quick move, faking him out as she took it in for a basket.

Chase took the rebound, but didn't shoot immediately. What had gotten into her? He'd never seen her so angry. So fiery. So beautiful. Her breasts moved freely under her T-shirt, and he was hard-pressed to pay attention to what she was saying. He took one step to the right, then shifted his weight, moved around her and fired a shot, making the basket.

She snagged the ball and dribbled it. "I was at home trying to figure out everything. I was upset. I was *wretched*. And you've been here having a good time with your friends! You were supposed to be thinking about our futures."

He stole the ball, making her move in to block his shot, toying with her. "First of all, I *was* miserable. I was so miserable I didn't even come home but went straight to your parents' house."

Her sneakers squealed on the hardwood floor as she stopped. "What?"

He sank a basket. The ball bounced away as they squared off with each other. "I went to talk to your parents. I told them everything. I apologized for my part in what happened to Brent. To all of you."

"What did they say?"

"That Brent had already told them about me. I'd just gotten here a few minutes before you. Gabe and Ben were already playing. We play every Sunday night, remember? I decided to join them for a minute before I showered and went to your place. But I wanted to celebrate with them. Unwind. Get myself under control."

"What were you celebrating?"

He pulled a piece of paper from his jeans' pocket and passed it to her. He watched as she unfolded it, saw her hands shake.

"'You have our blessing. Love, Mom, Dad and Brent.'" She pressed her fingers to her mouth and looked at him.

"I asked your parents for permission to marry you. I told them if they had any doubts, if they thought they couldn't welcome me into the family completely, that they should say so and I would walk away."

She shook her head weakly. He settled his hands on her shoulders.

"It was a lie, Tessa. I wouldn't have walked away. Between your house and theirs, I realized that I wasn't so noble after all. I want a family. I want you as my wife, and I want to have children with you. I want everything I didn't have. Everything I didn't think I deserved." He squeezed her shoulders. "Because I do. I do deserve you, and everything you offer me. Say something."

"I came here—" she swallowed "—because I was afraid I was making a mistake. That maybe I'd just convinced myself I was in love with you, had fantasized that we shared some kind of destiny."

"I love you, Tessa Rose. I don't have the slightest doubt of that." He drew her into his arms and held her close. Her hair smelled like a spring garden after a rainstorm. Her body felt familiar and magnificent and electrifying. "I don't know if I believe in destiny, but I do know that we waited for the right person and the right time—and *that* I believe in. With my whole heart, Tessa. My whole heart."

He drew back a little so that he could see her face. "If you have doubts, we can date. I don't blame you if you want to be courted. It's important, I gather. But you are going to marry me, sooner or later."

"Sooner or later?" Her voice hitched a little.

He couldn't read her expression. "Sooner, if you're pregnant."

"Oh."

Her face was still a blank, and he needed to know how much resistance he was encountering.

"I think you need a little convincing," he said, slipping his hands under her shirt and dragging the fabric up.

She grabbed his wrists. "Is this your idea of courting? I was thinking more along the lines of flowers and candy."

"I guarantee you it'll be sweet and satisfying. I love you, Tessa." He filled his hands with her breasts, dragged his thumbs across her hard nipples, smiled when she drew a quick breath.

"This is not playing fair," she murmured, but her eyes closed and she arched her back a little, which told him everything he needed.

He waited for her to say the words she'd said so many times to him, but she remained strangely silent. Insecurity tapped him on the shoulder. He ignored it. Instead he stripped off her T-shirt and enjoyed the way her cheeks flushed as she crossed her arms over her breasts and looked around.

"Chase! What if someone comes in?"

"The only people with keys..." He considered the thought a minute. "Maybe you're right. Don't move. And I mean don't move an inch or I won't be able to find you when I get back."

Tessa didn't budge as Chase walked across the gym then doused the lights. In a minute she would put him out of his misery. For the moment she was enjoying his efforts to convince her. She heard him walk toward her, but her eyes hadn't adjusted to the sudden darkness yet. Then silence descended. She couldn't hear him any longer.

"Chase?"

He didn't answer. Without warning, his arms came around her from behind, his hands cradled her breasts and she felt his body touch hers all the way to her feet—his naked body. His naked, aroused body. He nibbled her shoulder as he slid his hands under the waistband of her sweatpants. She groaned when he began to work his magic on her, the total darkness adding a whole new element.

"Marry me." His breath teased her ear, giving her chills. "I love you. Be mine forever, and I'll be yours."

"This is not courtship," she said, breathless. He was doing wonderful things to her, extraordinary, amazing, soul-satisfying things, with just his fingers and his mouth.

"I changed my mind. I can't wait."

"Yes," she said, simple and direct.

He stopped. "Yes? That worked? You'll marry me?"

She turned and looped her arms around his neck. "Something wrong with your hearing?"

He kissed her, long and deep and lovingly.

"I love you," she whispered against his mouth. "I never really believed I was making a mistake. I just needed to see you. To convince you that I was right. Your heart needs a woman's touch. I'm that woman."

"I know."

She smiled at the flash of ego. "I think you're going to make my life very interesting."

"I intend to try. I've got a thousand fantasies in mind for you."

"Been saving them up, have you?"

In a heartbeat he had her flat on her back. He tossed her shoes in different directions, peeled off her sweatpants and hurled them aside. He stretched out on her instantly, then sheathed himself within her with a slow, steady push.

"Fantasy number one," he murmured. "I want to hear you moan. I want to hear the sound echo all around us."

She smiled, confident of her power. "Make me."

He met the challenge. And when the echoing sounds faded to sighs he kissed her, grateful for everything she brought to his life—her tempting softness, her beautiful smile, her unwavering love.

"The minute I saw you, I knew you were going to change my life," he said.

"Destiny." Her tone of voice said she hadn't doubted it for a minute.

"I'm finally a believer, Miss Rose."

She ran a finger across his lips. "Do that again."

"What?"

"Smile. I love your smile."

"Make me."

Her grin turned decidedly wicked. She pushed him off her then stood. His eyes had adjusted enough to the darkness that he knew she'd walked toward the door, but her bare feet didn't make any sound. Then suddenly the lights came on and she strolled back to him, stooping to pick up the basketball along the way.

"One-on-one?" she asked, her brows arching in query.

He felt a smile tug at his mouth, stretching muscles he'd rarely used until recently.

"I'll even let you take some practice shots," he offered.

She laughed. "I'll bet."

He tucked his hands under his arms and clucked. And when her cheeks turned bright pink, he laughed.

"That's the sound *I* wanted to hear echo in this room, Chase Ryan. That was my fantasy."

"I think we're going to have to work on your fantasies. Maybe you just need a man's touch." He moved in on her, smiling as she bounced the ball, a direct challenge. "You know if someone climbs up a few feet outside any of the windows, they can see in."

He stole the ball from her as she stared, horrified, at the windows. She started to cover her body with her arms.

He dunked the ball. "You're so easy."

Laughter echoed, both masculine and feminine in pitch, the sound healing and celebrating. They didn't keep score, but Tessa insisted it was a tie. Chase smiled in agreement.

\* \* \* \* \*

*Don't miss Gabriel's Story ,*
**HIS SEDUCTIVE REVENGE,**
*available in June from Silhouette Desire®.*

### THE LIONESS TAMER Rebecca Brandewyne

*Man of the Month*

Tycoon Jordan Westcott was used to getting his own way. But then he went undercover in his family firm and met Mistral St Michel! He may have planned to tame this stubborn beauty, but was he falling under her spell instead?

### FIONA AND THE SEXY STRANGER Marie Ferrarella

*The Cutler Family*

When a stranger turned up on Fiona Reilly's doorstep with a bunch of flowers, she presumed he was the delivery man! When he asked her out to dinner, she thought he'd made a mistake. But, by the time handsome Henry Cutler proposed, she was ready to say yes!

### MILLIONAIRE DAD Leanne Banks

*The Rulebreakers*

Joe Caruthers had it all—success, wealth, dangerous good looks—and now, a woman pregnant with his child. Even though he wanted lovely Marley Fuller, a baby just *wasn't* in his plans—at least at first!

### THE COWBOY AND THE CALENDAR GIRL Nancy Martin

*Opposites Attract*

As soon as Carly Cortazzo saw handsome Hank Fowler's photograph, she felt an instant attraction. And he was even more gorgeous in real life! But did she and this rugged hunk have *anything* in common?

### THE RANCHER'S SPITTING IMAGE Peggy Moreland

*The McCloud Brides*

Jesse Barrister had returned home to find his former sweetheart Mandy McCloud had a child who was his spitting image. Now he wanted to claim the son he'd never known...*and* share a bed with Mandy.

### NON-REFUNDABLE GROOM Patty Salier

A dating service that *guaranteed* marriage—Elena Martin couldn't believe her luck when she was paired with sexy Garrett Sims. *She* was ready to say 'I do', but it seemed *he* had no intention of setting foot near an altar...

# COMING NEXT MONTH FROM

 **SILHOUETTE®**

## Sensation
*A thrilling mix of passion, adventure and drama*

**ROARKE'S WIFE** Beverly Barton
**WHILE SHE WAS SLEEPING** Diane Pershing
**PARTNERS IN PARENTHOOD** Raina Lynn
**UNDERCOVER COWBOY** Beverly Bird

## Intrigue
*Danger, deception and desire*

**UNFORGETTABLE NIGHT** Kelsey Roberts
**FRAMED** Karen Leabo
**A ONE-WOMAN MAN** M. L. Gamble
**FUGITIVE FATHER** Jean Barrett

## Special Edition
*Satisfying romances packed with emotion*

**OLDER, WISER...PREGNANT** Marilyn Pappano
**THE MAIL-ORDER MIX-UP** Pamela Toth
**THE COWBOY'S IDEAL WIFE** Victoria Pade
**HOT CHOCOLATE HONEYMOON** Cathy Gillen Thacker
**MEANT TO BE MARRIED** Ruth Wind
**THE BODYGUARD'S BRIDE** Jean Brashear

## books and a surprise gift!

We would like to take this opportunity to thank you for reading this Silhouette® book by offering you the chance to take FOUR more specially selected titles from the Desire™ series absolutely FREE! We're also making this offer to introduce you to the benefits of the Reader Service™—

* ★ FREE home delivery
* ★ FREE gifts and competitions
* ★ FREE monthly Newsletter
* ★ Exclusive Reader Service discounts
* ★ Books available before they're in the shops

Accepting these FREE books and gift places you under no obligation to buy, you may cancel at any time, even after receiving your free shipment. Simply complete your details below and return the entire page to the address below. *You don't even need a stamp!*

**YES!** Please send me 4 free Desire books and a surprise gift. I understand that unless you hear from me, I will receive 6 superb new titles every month for just £2.70 each, postage and packing free. I am under no obligation to purchase any books and may cancel my subscription at any time. The free books and gift will be mine to keep in any case.

D9EA

Ms/Mrs/Miss/Mr ..............................Initials.....................................
BLOCK CAPITALS PLEASE

Surname ...........................................................................................

Address ............................................................................................

...........................................................................................................

................................................................Postcode...............................

**Send this whole page to:**
THE READER SERVICE, FREEPOST CN81, CROYDON, CR9 3WZ
**(Eire readers please send coupon to: P.O. BOX 4546, DUBLIN 24.)**

Offer valid in UK and Eire only and not available to current Reader Service subscribers to this series. We reserve the right to refuse an application and applicants must be aged 18 years or over. Only one application per household. Terms and prices subject to change without notice. Offer expires 31st October 1999. As a result of this application, you may receive further offers from Harlequin Mills & Boon and other carefully selected companies. If you would prefer not to share in this opportunity please write to The Data Manager at the address above.

Silhouette is a registered trademark used under license.
Desire is being used as a trademark.

# HELEN R. MYERS

# Come Sundown

In the steamy heat of Parish, Mississippi, there is a new chief of police. Ben Rader is here to shape up the department, and first on the list is the investigation of a mysterious death.

But things are not what they appear to be. Come Sundown things change in Parish…